This is my story.

It really happened.

It's all true.

Not even the names have 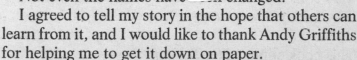 been changed.

I agreed to tell my story in the hope that others can learn from it, and I would like to thank Andy Griffiths for helping me to get it down on paper.

Like most people I took my bum for granted for too long. If this book can save even just one person from making the same mistake, then I will be happy.

Who knows?

The next bum it saves might be yours.

May your bum be with you always,

Zack Freeman

What People Have Said About *The Day My Bum Went Psycho*. (Honestly. Every word of it's true.)

'This book will be in the No. 2 slot by next week.'
The Sunday Business

'This book stinks.' *The Teleguff*

'Hilariass!' *Nicola Smells, Trumpedtown*

'Ten out of ten readers said their pants preferred it.'
A Talking Cat from Doggenham

'Fart? I nearly pooped!' *Jeremy Peedle*

'A book that registers over 5.5 on the Rectum Scale should be banned as unsuitable for children. This book registers 7.8.'
Giles Winterbottom, Letrip-on-Sea

'No ifs or butts – this book will crack you up!'
The Poos of the World

'Perfect reading for anyone with a loose end.'
John Bogg, Windchester

'A book that grips like buttocks on bran.'
The Times Dietary Supplement

Andy Griffiths is the popular and award-winning author of the *Just* series. He lives with his partner and two daughters in Melbourne, Australia, where he divides his time between story-writing and bum-fighting. *The Day My Bum Went Psycho* is his first novel and is based on a true story.

Also by Andy Griffiths
(illustrated by Terry Denton)

Just Kidding!
Just Annoying!
Just Stupid!
Just Crazy!

Visit Andy's Website:
www.andygriffiths.com.au

THE DAY
MY BUM WENT
PSYCHO

ANDY GRIFFITHS

MACMILLAN CHILDREN'S BOOKS

Teachers' notes for *The Day My Bum Went Psycho* are available at
www.panmacmillan.com.au and www.andygriffiths.com.au

First published 2001 by Pan Macmillan Australia Pty Limited

First published in the UK 2002 by Macmillan Children's Books
a division of Macmillan Publishers Limited
20 New Wharf Road, London N1 9RR
Basingstoke and Oxford
www.panmacmillan.com

Associated companies throughout the world

ISBN 0 330 40089 4

1 3 5 7 9 8 6 4 2

A CIP catalogue record for this book is available from
the British Library.

Typeset in 11.5/14pt Life Roman
Printed and bound in Great Britain by Mackays of Chatham plc, Kent

ACKNOWLEDGEMENTS

I am deeply grateful to Ian Smith for technical advice on the inner workings of volcanoes and Christian Doonan for technical advice on the chemical composition of flatulence.

I would also like to thank Jill Groves and Anna McFarlane for their tireless, painstaking and—it must be said—at times downright pedantic editing.

Above all I would like to thank Zack Freeman without whose courage this book would not have been possible, and without whose efforts we would probably all be walking around with bums for heads and heads for bums.

This book is not dedicated to my parents, by request—A.G.

This book is dedicated to my bum—Z.F.

CONTENTS

CHAPTER ONE

MIDNIGHT
BUM RALLY

Zack Freeman woke out of a deep sleep to see his bum perched on the ledge of his bedroom window. It was standing on two pudgy little legs, silhouetted against the moon, its little stick-like arms outstretched in front of it, as if it was about to dive.

Zack sat up in bed.

'No!' he yelled. 'Come back!'

But it was too late. His bum jumped out of the window and landed with a soft thud in the garden bed below.

Zack stared at the window and sighed.

'Oh no,' he said. 'Not again.'

This was not the first time Zack's bum had run away.

Since his twelfth birthday, two months ago, Zack's bum had made a habit of jumping off his body and running around the streets making a nuisance of itself. Zack was sick of it. So was the local bumcatcher who had already caught and impounded it three times.

Until recently Zack's bum had confined itself to a variety of harmless pranks, such as attaching itself to the faces of statues and passersby. But on its last outing it had joined a pack of five hundred feral bums who had lined the emergency stopping lane of the South Eastern Freeway and mooned all the people driving to work. This stunt had caused many accidents, which the bums had thought was a great laugh. The sentencing judge, however, was not amused and placed them all on twelve month good behaviour bonds.

Zack knew he had to catch his bum himself this time. If the bumcatcher got involved, he would have to report it and Zack's bum would end up in jail for sure. And there was no way Zack wanted to spend every second weekend visiting his bum in jail.

Zack threw back the blankets and was about to get out of bed when he heard his grandmother call out from the next room.

'Zack?' she said. 'Is that you?'

'Yes, Gran,' said Zack. 'It's all right, go back to sleep.'

'What was that noise?' said his gran. 'Have they resumed firing?'

Zack rolled his eyes.

'There's no war, Gran,' he said. 'Go back to sleep.'

Zack was living with his grandmother while his parents were away. They both played in the wind section of the National Symphony Orchestra and went on tour three or four times a year, during which Zack would have to stay with his grandmother—sometimes for up to a month at a time. He

loved his grandmother, but sometimes he wondered who was looking after who.

'No war?' said his grandmother. 'You mean the war's over?'

'Yes,' said Zack.

He was used to this conversation. She was always talking about the war. Zack wasn't sure which war she was talking about, or how long ago it had happened, or whether it had even happened at all—all he knew was that it seemed real to her.

'Did we win?'

'Yes, Gran,' said Zack. He figured that she would go back to sleep quicker if he just agreed with everything she said. 'We creamed them.'

'That's good,' said his grandmother. 'I'll take over the watch. You get some rest. You've earned it, soldier.'

'Yes, Gran,' said Zack.

He couldn't tell her the truth. It would be bad enough talking to his parents about his bum, let alone his grandmother.

He waited a minute until he could hear her snoring and then he got out of bed. With difficulty. It wasn't that easy moving without a bum. Zack walked across the room to the window, leaned out and peered into the night.

He saw his bum standing on the tips of its toes at the end of the driveway, as if sniffing the air. It was looking up and down the street.

There was still time to catch it. But he'd have to be quick.

Zack climbed out of the window and tiptoed down the driveway.

As he got closer, Zack realised that he wasn't the only one trying to catch his bum.

Mittens, his grandmother's cat, was crouched on top of the front fence, ready to pounce.

'Uh-oh,' said Zack. He wasn't sure who was in more danger—Mittens or his bum. Mittens was always catching birds and mice and leaving them half-chewed on the front doorstep. But she had never caught a bum before. Well, not as far as Zack knew, anyway. And a half-chewed bum on the doorstep wouldn't be something you'd be likely not to notice. Still, he didn't want to take any chances.

Before Zack had time to do anything, however, Mittens leapt.

But Zack's bum was faster.

It bent over, aimed itself directly at Mittens, and fired a loud, deadly stream of gas. Mittens fell to the ground. Zack's bum took off up the street, its little arms and legs pumping away like pistons.

Zack was shocked. He knew that his bum had gone feral, but he'd never seen it kill anything before. He had to get it back. He knew that once a bum gets a taste for killing, it is very difficult for them to stop.

But first he had to try to help Mittens.

Zack hobbled over to her body and knelt down. Poor Mittens was in a bad way. Zack pulled her head back, pinched her nostrils and was preparing to give her mouth-to-mouth resuscitation when Mittens coughed.

She wasn't dead after all. She had just been stunned.

Zack breathed a sigh of relief.

'So my bum isn't a killer,' he thought. 'Not yet, anyway.'

In the distance he could see the dark shape of his bum disappearing over the top of the hill.

He got up, pulled the cord of his pyjama pants as tight as possible, and ran after it.

As he ran, Zack cursed his luck. All he wanted was a bum that would settle down and just be a bum. A bum that wouldn't embarrass him in public at every possible opportunity. A bum that wouldn't make rude comments whenever he tried to talk to girls. At the very least he'd settle for a bum that didn't jump off his body and gas cats in the middle of the night.

By the time Zack got to the top of the hill his bum was already halfway down the other side, heading towards the local football stadium.

And it wasn't the only one either.

Zack couldn't believe what he was seeing.

There were bums everywhere. Pouring into the stadium from all directions.

It was an amazing sight.

Bums.

Hundreds of them.

Thousands.

Big bums.

Small bums.

Fat bums.

Scrawny bums.

Pimply bums.

Hairy bums.

Big wobbly bums tottering along on tiny white legs. Tiny babies' bums crawling across the ground.

Every sort of bum you could imagine was heading towards the stadium.

Zack was amazed. He'd never seen so many bums without their owners attached. But why? he wondered. What was going on?

Zack crept quietly down the hill in the darkness and crossed the road to the wooden fence surrounding the stadium. A large group of bums was approaching him from the left. Big bums. And they looked mean. Zack looked around for somewhere to hide. On the other side of the stadium was a large grandstand, but it was too far away. To his right, however, there was a small wooden hotdog stand. Zack hesitated. The bums were getting close. He dived over the counter.

The group of bums passed by him, muttering excitedly. Zack couldn't understand what they were saying, but he could smell it all right.

He didn't dare to poke his head up for at least five minutes after they had passed. When he finally did look out he was shocked.

In front of him was a sea of bums. Bums filled every available bit of space in the stadium, as well as the grandstand on the far side.

Zack looked for his bum but couldn't pick it out from the crowd.

It didn't really have any distinguishing features apart from the fact that it was small and pink.

But as he looked, the crowd began to part. And gasp.

'Look! There he is!' said one bum.

'It's him!' said another.

'Our leader,' said a third.

For a moment Zack thought they were talking about him, but then he realised they were looking past the hotdog stand. He turned around and strained to catch a glimpse of whoever or whatever it was they were looking at, but there were too many bums in the way.

And then he saw it.

It was a bum.

But not just any bum.

It was small and pink and strangely familiar.

It was *his* bum.

Zack couldn't believe it.

He watched as his bum made its way through the crowd. It passed directly in front of the hotdog stand. As it passed, the other bums would reach out and try to touch it like it was some kind of celebrity. Occasionally Zack's bum would touch one of the hands extended towards it, but mostly it was protected by a group of four bumguards. Two walked in front of it, pushing aside any bum that tried to get too close. The other two followed a few paces behind, protecting it from the rear.

Zack's bum reached the scoreboard, climbed up a small ladder and then walked across a narrow platform that ran along the bottom.

When it reached the middle of the platform it stopped.

The bumguards remained on the ground and formed a line to keep the crowd from surging forwards.

One of the guards was shining a torch on Zack's

bum. The light shining on it from below made it look quite sinister.

Zack wiped his brow.

'This can't be happening,' he said to himself. 'It can't be happening. It can't be happening.'

But it *was* happening.

Zack's bum raised a bum-trumpet to its mouth and blew a long loud note.

The whole crowd became silent.

Then Zack's bum began to speak.

'Brothers and sisters,' it said quietly. 'You know why I have called you here, so let me get straight to the point. For too long we have been forced to do the dirty work for the human race. For too long we have been laughed at, smacked, pinched, kicked, sat on and generally regarded as figures of fun! For too long we have been denied our rightful place on top of the neck where we belong!'

There was an enormous cheer from the crowd.

Zack blocked his nose and wiped his eyes. When one bum talks it's bad enough, but when thousands talk at the same time, well, it's not pleasant to say the least.

After a few minutes the cheering died down.

'But what can we do?' said a bony bum in the front row. 'We're just bums.'

Zack's bum stepped to the edge of the platform, the torchlight making it look more sinister than ever.

'No, my friend,' it said. 'Divided we are just bums, but united we have the potential to be the most powerful force on the planet. Right now, on an island in the Sea of Bums, bums from all over

the world are working around the clock to fill an extinct volcano. When it is full, it will become the greatest bumcano in the history of the world. And when it erupts it will be devastating enough to knock out every human being on Earth.'

Zack's bum paused, enjoying the dramatic effect its words had on the assembled bummery.

'That, my brothers and sisters,' it said, 'will be when we strike. We will swap places with the heads and assume our rightful position on top of the neck. By the time the humans come to, the Age of Bums will have begun and there will be nothing anybody can do to stop us!'

The bums began cheering again.

Zack lowered himself behind the counter and grimaced, trying to make sense of his bum's crazy plan. Bums taking the place of heads? Heads taking the place of bums?

The idea made Zack's stomach turn.

His bum had to be stopped. He had to tell the local bumcatcher what was going on. Even if it meant that his bum would end up in jail.

But how could he get to the bumcatcher? wondered Zack. He was stuck in a hotdog stand surrounded by thousands of deranged bums. He wasn't going anywhere.

He peeked over the top of the counter.

Just then a bum ran screaming through the gates.

Followed by the bumcatcher.

'Help!' called the bum. 'He's got a bum-magnet!'

The bumcatcher was holding what looked like a mini satellite dish in his outstretched hand. But as he

entered the stadium he stopped dead in his tracks, obviously stunned by the huge number of bums in front of him. He dropped the bum-magnet and started to back away. But it was too late. The bums closed in all around him.

'Please, no!' he begged. 'Let me go!'

'Bring him to me,' commanded Zack's bum.

Two of the bumguards shoved their way through the crowd and Zack watched in horror as the bumguards grabbed the bumcatcher and dragged him, kicking and struggling, back towards the scoreboard.

'Help!' yelled the bumcatcher as the bumguards dragged him up the ladder and onto the platform where Zack's bum was standing.

The sight of the bumcatcher seemed to enrage the bums. They were booing and hissing. The air stank with their poisonous fumes. Brown blobs were flying through the air and splattering onto the back of the scoreboard.

The bumguards dropped the bumcatcher on the platform in front of Zack's bum and moved away.

Zack wondered whether he should try to help him, but he was too scared. There must have been more than ten thousand bums out there. Even supposing that he could convince his own bum to give up its plans for world domination—and that was a big 'if'— he didn't like his chances of trying to convince the other bums. They were in an ugly mood. And judging by the smell in the air, getting uglier by the minute.

'Stand up, bumcatcher,' said Zack's bum.

The bumcatcher slowly stood up. His legs were trembling.

'Let me go,' he gasped. 'Please.'

'Why would I do that?' said Zack's bum. 'So you can catch us all?'

'I was only trying to help you,' said the bumcatcher.

'Help us?' said Zack's bum. 'And how exactly were you trying to help us? By sucking us up with your bum-magnet? By shooting us with your bum-guns? By holding us in your cages like common criminals?'

'All I'm interested in is trying to get bums back to their owners,' said the bumcatcher. 'It's my job.'

Zack's bum turned to the crowd.

'Owners,' it spat. 'Owners! Did you hear that? That is exactly what this rally is all about. Bums are not slaves. We are not owned by anybody!'

'But a bum without an owner is just a . . . a . . . a bum,' said the bumcatcher.

At that the bums resumed their boos and hisses and launched a fresh round of missiles at the bumcatcher.

Zack's bum turned to the crowd and put its hands up.

'Enough,' it said.

Then it turned back to the bumcatcher and touched his shoulder.

'I'm sorry you feel that way,' it said. 'But that's understandable. After all, it's your head talking—not your bum. But we can fix that.'

The bumcatcher's eyes widened.

'Surely you don't mean . . . no . . . you can't be serious!'

Zack's bum nodded.

'That's exactly what I mean. But don't be scared. Think of it as an honour. You will be the first of the

new order. The first to be "rearranged". What do you say?'

Without waiting for an answer, Zack's bum motioned to the bumguards.

They swung into action.

One of them produced a pair of scissors, cut a hole in the back of the bumcatcher's trousers and removed his bum.

It came out coughing. It was very white and, judging by the way it was shivering, very frightened.

'It's okay, little fella,' said Zack's bum, patting it. 'You'll be all right.'

Meanwhile the other bumguard grabbed a handful of the bumcatcher's hair and began to pull it.

The bumcatcher yelled.

'I can't do it,' said the bum. 'I need help!'

One of the other bumguards put its arms around the first bum and they both started pulling.

All of a sudden the bumcatcher's head came free. The bumguards stumbled backwards and fell over.

'Well don't just lie there,' said Zack's bum, taking the head of the bumcatcher from the bumguard. 'Stand him up!'

The bumguards picked the bumcatcher up off the platform and helped him to his feet. He stood there, swaying groggily back and forth while Zack's bum attached the bumcatcher's head to where his bum had been.

The crowd cheered.

But that cheer was nothing compared to the cheer when Zack's bum, lifted up by two of the bumguards, crowned the bumcatcher's neck with his bum.

'All hail the new order!' Yelled Zack's bum.

'ALL HAIL THE NEW ORDER!' chanted the crowd.

It was a truly grotesque sight. The bumcatcher swayed from side to side, as if his bum wasn't sure how to control its new body.

'Help!' yelled the bumcatcher's head. 'I can't breathe!'

'Now you know how we feel,' said Zack's bum. 'Guards—put his underpants back on!'

The bums pulled the bumcatcher's underpants up over his face, muffling any further protests.

After this, Zack's bum turned back to the crowd.

'This is just the beginning,' it yelled. 'Follow me now! To the bumcano! To our glorious future!'

Zack's bum leapt off the platform and crowd-surfed its way to the main exit.

'To the bumcano!' it cried as it passed through the gate.

'To the bumcano!' echoed the vast crowd of bums as they followed it into the night.

Zack waited until all the bums had left the stadium. He was terrified. He didn't want what had happened to the bumcatcher to happen to him. He probably would have waited longer except that the bumcatcher's body, still swaying on the platform, took a few uncertain steps forward and fell.

Zack heard the bumcatcher groan. He jumped out of the hotdog stand and ran to him.

The bumcatcher's bum was scared.

'I didn't want this,' it whimpered.

'I know,' said Zack. 'I saw the whole thing.'

Zack pulled the bumcatcher's underpants down so that he could see the bumcatcher's face.

He looked terrible. His face was bright red, his eyes popping out of their sockets ... and his breath was shocking. To make things worse he was poking his tongue out and making a loud slobbery raspberry noise.

He was clearly delirious. Whether it was from the rearrangement or the fall was hard to say, but Zack knew he had to try to bring him to his senses.

Zack took a can of pine-scented air-freshener that was hanging off the bumcatcher's belt and sprayed it near his face to try to neutralise the effects of the rearrangement. As the smell of pine trees filled the air, the bumcatcher's eyeballs stopped rolling and he focused.

'Zack?' he said, with fresh terror in his eyes. 'What are you doing here? You're not on their side, are you?'

'No way,' said Zack. 'I was following my bum. It sneaked out of my bedroom.'

The bumcatcher groaned.

'That was your bum up there, wasn't it?' he said.

'Yes,' said Zack, feeling ashamed.

'I thought I recognised it,' said the bumcatcher. 'I never forget a bum.'

'You look bad,' said Zack, quickly changing the subject. 'Do you think you'll be able to catch them?'

The bumcatcher shook his head.

'I'm going to be out of action for a while,' he said.

'At least until I get myself sorted out. I can't stop those bums now.'

'But if you can't, then who will?' said Zack.

The bumcatcher winced as he spoke.

'Listen to me, Zack,' he said. 'Your bum has gone psycho. There's only one person who can stop it . . . Silas Sterne.'

'Silas Sterne?' said Zack.

The bumcatcher nodded.

Zack knew about Silas Sterne. Everybody did. Like all his friends at school, Zack collected bum-fighter trading cards, and the card featuring Silas Sterne was the rarest and the most prized of them all. He was one of the world's greatest bum hunters. He'd hunted—and captured—some of the biggest and meanest bums on the planet. His photograph on the card showed a fierce-looking man dressed in a shiny black Ninja suit. Unlike a Ninja, however, he was wearing a white hard hat with a miner's lamp on the front of it. Also, unlike a Ninja, he had a couple of massive bum-guns slung across his shoulders. Zack had had to trade ten of his best bum-fighter cards for it, including the cards featuring the Smacker, the Kicker and the Kisser, but he was so happy to get the Silas Sterne card he didn't even mind.

The bumcatcher groaned. His eyes were closed.

He was obviously in pain.

Zack sprayed a little more air-freshener above his head.

The bumcatcher opened his eyes and focused on him with difficulty.

'Zack, you have to go to the Bum Hunter. Tell him

everything that's happened here tonight. He'll know what to do.'

'But I can't go out there,' said Zack. 'It's too dangerous. The whole town will be crawling with bums.'

'Zack,' said the bumcatcher, 'it's *your* bum. It's *your* responsibility. You can't stick your head in the sand, or it will end up grafted to your backside—just like mine.'

He was right. Zack knew that. But he was still scared. Despite his enthusiasm for collecting bum-fighter trading cards he had no desire to be a bum-fighter himself. Well, perhaps it wasn't so much a lack of desire as a lack of aptitude. Zack had failed the Junior Bum-fighters' League entry exam three times. Each time he'd been gassed by a partic-ularly clumsy and slow-moving bum, much to the amusement of the other junior bum-fighters and the embarrassment of his parents and himself. After the third gassing he'd given up all thoughts of fighting bums and devoted himself to his trading card col-lection instead.

The bumcatcher, sensing Zack's fear, spoke to him gently.

'Look, Zack,' he said, 'I'm not asking you to fight them. All you have to do is to contact the Bum Hunter. Here, I've got everything you need. My utility belt. Take it.'

The bumcatcher undid the belt from around his waist and handed it to Zack.

Zack took the belt. It was made of thick brown leather and had a large gold buckle with the words

'BE BOLD, BE BRAVE, BE FREE' inscribed on the front. The belt had a variety of little holsters and hooks to which all the basic tools of bum-catching were attached. There were three wooden clothes-pegs, a roll of toilet paper, a fluffy pink toilet seat cover, a small rolled up net, a row of corks, a set of sewing needles, a box of matches, a tennis racquet and a cake of soap.

Zack understood what most of the items were for, except the soap.

'What's the soap for?' he asked.

'For washing your hands,' said the bumcatcher. 'It's the first rule of bum-fighting. Always wash your hands afterwards. Got that?'

Zack nodded.

The bumcatcher lay back down, grimacing with pain.

'And one more thing, Zack,' he murmured weakly.

'What's that?' said Zack, his mind reeling.

'Put these socks on.'

The bumcatcher handed him a pair of thick brown bumcatcher socks.

'Socks?' said Zack, wondering if the bumcatcher had gone mad.

'Yes,' said the bumcatcher. 'Put them on now, and don't take them off until you need them.'

'How will I know when I need them?' said Zack, still confused.

'You'll know,' he said. 'You'll just know.'

'Where will I find the Bum Hunter?' asked Zack.

The bumcatcher didn't respond. He'd lost consciousness.

Zack slapped his cheek. 'Wake up!' he said. 'You haven't told me where I can find the Bum Hunter.'

For a moment there was no response.

Then the bumcatcher half-opened his eyes.

He tried to form words. '. . . I . . . need . . . more . . . spray . . .' he whispered.

Zack sprayed.

The bumcatcher started talking although still with difficulty.

'You'll . . . find . . . him . . . at . . . the . . . the . . .'

His voice trailed off.

Zack pressed the nozzle on the spray can, but nothing happened. He pressed it again. Still nothing.

Zack threw the can on the ground.

'Where!?' he pleaded. 'Just tell me where!!!'

But it was no use. The bumcatcher was completely out of it.

Zack looked at the belt in his hand and read the inscription on the buckle again.

BE BOLD. BE BRAVE. BE FREE.

Zack didn't feel bold.

He didn't feel brave.

And he certainly didn't feel free.

He wasn't free to live his life.

His bum was always wrecking everything.

Whatever he tried to do his bum would always find some way to sabotage it.

Zack knew that the bumcatcher was right.

His bum was his responsibility. He had to find the Bum Hunter before it got any more out of control.

Zack put the belt on. It hung loosely around his waist. He pulled it tight but it still felt weird. It

reminded him of the feeling he'd had when he'd put on the cowboy suit his parents had given him for his sixth birthday. It was too big and the seams had itched against his skin. To make things worse he'd pricked himself with the shiny silver Sheriff's badge and cried. He'd begged to be able to take it off, much to his father's frustration. 'But you only just put it on!' he'd said. 'Give him time,' said his mother. 'He probably just needs to grow into it.' But Zack had never worn it again. He just didn't like it. And he didn't like the belt. As far as Zack was concerned, the only difference between his cowboy suit and the bumcatcher's belt was that instead of guns he had a roll of toilet paper on one hip and a tennis racquet on the other.

Just as Zack was about to leave, he remembered the socks.

'Oh great,' he mumbled as he rolled them onto his feet. 'Not only do I have to find the Bum Hunter, get my crazy bum back and save the world, I have to wear bumcatcher socks that will make my feet all hot and stinky. This day just keeps getting better and better.'

He pulled his shoes back on and headed towards the gate.

CHAPTER TWO

THE BUM HUNTER'S DAUGHTER

Zack couldn't see a single bum anywhere as he left the stadium.

But he could see where they'd been.

There were skidmarks everywhere. Splintered, broken, smoking trees. Smashed house windows. The road pockmarked with more craters and blast holes than the surface of the moon. Cars lying on their sides or completely overturned, obviously shaken by some powerful blasts.

And everywhere, permeating everything, the air was warm and thick with the stench of rotten-egg gas. Breathing was almost impossible.

Zack reached down to the belt, took out one of the clothespegs and put it on his nose. It provided instant relief. He was glad that the bumcatcher had insisted he take the belt.

As he crossed a large intersection on the outskirts of town he noticed a droning noise.

Zack couldn't identify it, but it was getting louder. It seemed to be coming from overhead.

He looked up. The sky was streaked with light. Dawn was not far away.

And then he saw them.

Flying bums.

A whole squadron.

Heading straight towards him.

The noise was deafening and the smell was so intense that Zack almost passed out.

He ran down a hill to hide under some trees beside a small creek, but it was too late.

They'd seen him.

As Zack ran, he looked over his shoulder. A bum broke away from the pack and began to zoom towards him.

It was not a pretty sight.

It was huge, and coming in fast.

Zack fell to the ground and put his hands over his head—just in time. The bum swooped down over the top of him, brushing the back of his hands. Zack lifted his head to see the bum shoot up into the sky, turn and start hurtling towards him, even faster this time.

Zack gulped.

This was just like the exam he'd failed the last time he'd tried out for the Junior Bum-fighters' League. Except worse. The bum that had gassed him there was slow-moving and clumsy. This bum was bigger and meaner and meant business. Real business.

Zack became aware of a sharp pain in his side. It was the tennis racquet handle. He pushed himself

up onto one elbow, reached down and pulled the racquet out of the belt. If he was going to die, he at least wanted to die in comfort.

Then Zack noticed a strange thing.

As he produced the tennis racquet from underneath him the colour drained from the bum, leaving it a deathly white.

Instinctively, Zack realised that the bum was scared.

It was scared of the racquet!

Zack gripped the handle tightly and a daring idea formed in his mind.

He could hit it.

It was worth a try. After all, what did he have to lose? He figured he was about to die anyway.

Zack rolled over, sat up and hid the racquet behind his back. He waited until the bum was almost on top of him, and then he let fly.

THWACK!

The bum went hurtling off his racquet and into the back of a parked car.

BOOM!

The explosion was deafening and the force of it knocked Zack over onto his back.

Zack couldn't believe what he'd just done.

He stood up to run, but two more bums, even larger than the first, broke away from the main group and sped towards him. Zack raised his tennis racquet, ready to hit them. As they drew closer, however, one veered around to attack him from behind while the other continued its assault from the front.

Zack gulped. And gulped again.

One gulp for each bum.

Those bums were smart, he thought. They knew he could hit only one at a time.

But then Zack had another daring idea.

He focused his eyes on the bum coming towards him.

He could hear the evil drone of the other bum coming in from behind.

At the last possible moment he ducked.

The bums collided with a thunderous sonic boom.

Zack was thrown face first onto the ground.

But that wasn't the end of his problems because now the rest of the squadron was heading towards him.

And they weren't happy.

Zack knew his tennis racquet would be no use against that many bums. There must have been at least fifty of them spread out across the sky and heading in at him from every direction.

He didn't know a lot about bum-fighting, but he knew enough to know what this meant.

It was a cluster bum.

Zack started running.

He had to find cover or he was going to be obliterated.

And then Zack saw it . . . an open storm drain.

He ran towards it.

He'd made it to the mouth of the enormous pipe when the bums collided.

WHAM!

He felt the heat on his back as the blast propelled him into the darkness of the drain.

Zack rocketed through the pipe and shot out into a large open area into which a number of other drains emptied.

He crashed onto a small card table surrounded by bums. The table collapsed underneath him and the bums went flying. But before Zack could get up, the bums were all around him, poking him with their soft, frog-like fingers.

'Well, well, well,' said a well-scrubbed bum who was wearing a cardboard party hat in the shape of a crown. 'If it isn't a bumcatcher! How nice of him to drop in, isn't it, Maurice?'

Maurice, a larger bum standing beside him, nodded.

'Very nice, Prince,' he said in a deep voice. 'Very, very nice indeed.'

The rest of the bums elbowed one another and sniggered.

The bum called Prince jumped up onto Zack's chest.

'Well?' he said. 'To what do we owe this unexpected pleasure, bumcatcher?'

The smell of the Prince's breath almost knocked Zack out, despite the clothespeg on his nose.

'I'm not a bumcatcher,' said Zack.

'Do you take me for a fool?' said the Prince.

'No,' said Zack.

'Then why do you insult me?' said the Prince.

'Insult you?' said Zack. 'What do you mean?'

'Well, you're wearing a bumcatcher's utility belt,' said the Prince reaching forward, unclipping the belt and dangling it in front of Zack's face. 'I assume you're not delivering pizzas.'

The other bums slapped their thighs and winked at one another in appreciation of their leader's joke.

'That's not my belt,' said Zack.

'Look,' said the Prince, 'I'd like to believe you. I really would, wouldn't I, Maurice?'

'That's right,' said Maurice. 'He would. He really would. He really and truly . . .'

'That will do, Maurice,' said the Prince.

'Sorry, sir,' said Maurice.

'As I was saying,' said the Prince, 'I would like to believe you, but it's more than my job's worth, you see. As leader of Bum Intelligence it's my job to capture and interrogate any humans engaged in anti-bum activities. Now put yourself in my shoes. A human wearing a bumcatcher's utility belt enters the room and tells us that he's not a bumcatcher. What would you do?'

'Let him go?' suggested Zack.

'No,' said the Prince. 'I hoped you might be a little more clever than that. I would interrogate him. Find out who he's working for and how many more of them there are. I'd probably even have to torture him, unless he wanted to save time and tell me the truth straight up.'

As the Prince spoke, the gang of bums closed in even more tightly around Zack.

'I'm telling you,' said Zack, 'I'm not a bum-catcher and I don't work for anyone.'

But the Prince ignored him.

'Maurice?' he said.

Maurice stepped forward, snapping his feet to attention.

'Yes, sir!'

'Match, please,' said the Prince.

'Yes, sir!' said Maurice producing a box of matches. He opened the box and passed a match to the Prince.

'Know what this is?' said the Prince, waving it in front of Zack's face.

The gang of bums all took a few steps back.

'Yes,' said Zack, beginning to tremble. 'A match.'

'Good,' said the Prince. 'At last we're getting somewhere. Now tell me, who are you working for?'

'Nobody,' said Zack. 'You're making a mistake. I'm not working for anybody. I'm a civilian.'

The Prince nodded.

For a moment Zack thought it was because he'd understood.

But then the Prince gestured to Maurice to come closer.

Maurice stepped forward with the matchbox held out in his hand.

'I was hoping to avoid this,' said the Prince in a low voice. 'But unless you answer my questions truthfully you leave me no choice.'

'I am telling you the truth,' said Zack, feeling the sweat form on the back of his neck. The Prince was clearly psycho, he thought. Perhaps even more psycho than his own bum.

The Prince sighed and struck the match against the box. It flared.

The bums all leaned forward as close as they dared, not wanting to miss a single moment of the action.

Zack knew what was coming.

Burns and matches were a bad combination.

He tried to get away but Maurice put his foot on his chest.

Zack was trapped.

The Prince took a deep breath, brought the match in front of his mouth and held out his finger.

'Maurice—pull my finger,' he said.

Zack closed his eyes.

Suddenly he heard a splash.

'Stop right there!' said a voice. 'Move away from him and face the wall. That goes for all of you.'

Zack looked up.

There, standing at the end of the drain he'd slid through, was a girl wearing army camouflage pants and a green top. Her hair was a tangled mess. She looked like she'd been living rough. She was heavily armed: a bum-gun on each hip, a knife strapped to one of her black combat boots and a huge bumblaster hanging off her shoulder. She was holding onto it with both hands, standing absolutely still, with the air of somebody who expected to be obeyed. She was scowling, looking directly at the Prince, who hadn't moved.

'Well, what are you waiting for?' she said, jumping

down from the lip of the pipe and landing cat-like on the metal grate without losing either her balance or her poise.

The bums all scuttled to the edge of the drain. All except for the Prince and Maurice.

'Dear me,' said the Prince. 'Such rudeness. Have you ever heard the like, Maurice?'

'No, sir,' said Maurice gravely, 'I don't believe I have.'

'You, my dear,' said the Prince, turning to the girl, 'need to learn some manners.'

'And you need to move to that wall,' she said, taking a menacing step towards him, 'or I will shoot.'

'I will do as you ask,' said the Prince. 'But first you must say "please".'

The only response from the girl was a volley of gun fire. Drawing-pins shot out of her gun and embedded themselves in a straight line along the table-top, stopping only a few centimetres from Zack's leg.

Maurice screamed.

'I used drawing-pins that time,' said the girl. 'Next time it will be staples.'

'Okay, all right,' said the Prince. 'Temper, temper!'

Zack reached up and snatched the utility belt from the Prince's hand.

The Prince glanced at the girl, looking slightly worried.

'We weren't going to hurt him,' he said, looking back at Zack. 'Honestly. We were just having a bit of fun weren't we, Maurice?'

Suddenly the air was full of staples. The girl sprayed the metal grate in front of the Prince and

Maurice. They shielded themselves as best they could with their little froggy arms, but many of the staples rebounded and stuck into them.

They responded by jumping around as if they were standing on a hotplate.

'Hey!' said the Prince. 'That hurts!'

'Just shut up and move,' said the girl. 'I won't tell you again. Next time it will be nails. Rusty ones.'

Something about her tone, combined with the threat of rusty nails, was serious enough to get through to the Prince and Maurice. They ran to join the other bums at the far side of the drain.

The girl walked towards Zack, staring angrily into his eyes. Zack was sweating. She was almost more frightening than the bums.

'Are you hurt?' said the girl.

'No,' said Zack. 'You came just in time.'

'I heard the cluster bum,' she said. 'I figured they must have been after somebody. What the hell were you doing out after a bum-siren had been sounded anyway?'

'Bum-siren?' said Zack. 'I didn't hear a bum-siren.'

'You must be deaf as well as dumb,' she said.

'What?' Zack was beginning to think the Prince was right. This girl *was* rude.

'Anyone who walks around the streets in the middle of a bum curfew, unarmed, is asking for trouble,' she said. 'And then I have to waste my time saving them.'

'I wasn't unarmed,' said Zack, showing her the utility belt. 'I was wearing this.'

'That's a cute little toy,' the girl said, smiling. 'Did you get it for Christmas?'

'No,' said Zack. 'A bumcatcher gave it to me.'

The girl sighed.

'Bloody street cleaners,' she said. 'They should leave it to the professionals.'

'He is a professional,' said Zack.

'If God had meant us to *catch* bums,' she said, patting her bumblaster, 'she wouldn't have given us these to kill them with.'

'So you're a . . .'

'Bum-fighter,' she said.

'What's your name?' said Zack.

'Eleanor.'

'I'm Zack,' he said, holding out his hand.

She ignored it.

'Let's get out of here,' she said. 'It stinks.'

She waved her gun towards the pipe she'd jumped down from.

'Can you get up there?'

'I think so,' said Zack.

'Let's go then,' she said. She turned, ran towards the wall, and in one graceful move, jumped and landed back up on the ledge of the drain.

Zack went as far back as he could and began to run. He jumped, reached up for the lip of the drain and missed. He put his hands on the ledge and tried to pull himself up. He got his head and shoulders into the pipe, but it was hard to get a good grip on the slippery concrete.

Eleanor knelt down and grabbed Zack's pyjama top.

With one mighty heave she swung him up over the drain lip and into the pipe. She did it with such force that Zack went sliding along the pipe through the darkness and shot out the other end, where he'd originally come in.

Eleanor was right behind him.

'Come on,' she said as they emerged, blinking, into the light. 'My bum-mobile is hidden in a park not far from here.'

'You've got a bum-mobile?' said Zack. 'What sort?'

'A 370-TZ.'

'With retractable wings?' he said.

'Of course,' she said. 'Handles all terrain. Even goes underwater.'

'Wow,' said Zack. He looked at the girl. She couldn't have been much older than him and yet she already had her own bum-mobile.

The girl took one of her bum-guns from her holster and handed it to him.

'Here,' she said, 'you'd better take this.'

Zack looked at the gun and felt his pulse quickening. It was a 4502-LL. The LL stood for Laxative Launcher. State of the art. It could fire up to five capsules of pure laxative per second.

'Are you sure?' he said.

'Of course I'm sure,' she said. 'What's the matter—are you scared?'

'No,' said Zack quickly. Up until now he had only read about guns like this. He'd never dreamed he'd ever actually get to hold one.

He held the gun up to his eye, put his finger on the trigger and took aim through the telescopic viewfinder.

Suddenly the gun jolted backwards in his hands and a volley of capsules poured out of its neck.

'You idiot!' said Eleanor. 'Are you trying to get us killed?'

'I'm sorry,' he said. 'It was an accident.'

'You'll have to be more careful than that if you want to stay alive,' she said. 'Let's go. And keep your head down. I can't see any bums, but that doesn't mean they're not around.'

Zack nodded, his face burning with embarrassment. He knew he was no bum-fighter, but it was too late to back out now.

Crouching low, Zack followed the girl through the long grass by the side of the creek. Soon they reached the edge of a large park.

Eleanor pointed to a weeping willow on the other side. Its thick branches drooped all the way to the ground.

'That's where the bum-mobile is hidden,' she said. 'Let's go.'

Zack nodded.

They were about halfway across the park when they heard a weird high-pitched squealing noise above them.

'What's that?' said Zack.

'Get down!' said Eleanor, pushing him roughly to the ground.

A bum whizzed over their heads and splattered onto the ground a few metres in front of them.

'Kamikaze bums!' said Eleanor, pointing to a large dead tree behind them—its branches lined with hundreds of bums, each wearing a red band. 'We're going to have to make a run for it.'

She sprinted off across the park towards the bum-mobile. Zack ran after her. The bums whizzed and whined overhead, exploding all around them.

Finally they made it to the willow tree.

Eleanor parted the curtain of branches to reveal the bum-mobile.

Zack's eyes bulged. The 370-TZ was an amazing machine. It resembled an armoured tank, except it was as if the top half had been removed and replaced with two large perspex domes.

Also, unlike a tank, it had a long yellow nose out the front of it tapering to a very sharp point. The letters 'BH-007' were written along the side in red. But the thing that really caught Zack's eye were the three rocket thrusters mounted at the rear. This would make the bum-mobile capable of flying at least twice the speed of wind—easily enough to hunt down or, if necessary, escape from the biggest and meanest of bums.

Zack was so amazed at the sight of the bum-mobile that he forgot about the bum-gun in his hand. Suddenly another volley of capsules sprayed out of the neck and into the trunk of the tree.

For a moment nothing happened, and then Zack saw the most incredible thing he had ever seen. Every single leaf fell off the tree, leaving just a skeleton of branches and the bum-mobile completely exposed. Zack blinked and shook his head. They were powerful laxatives, that was for sure.

'You idiot!' yelled Eleanor. 'Now look what you've done!'

'It was an accident,' said Zack, but he was drowned

out by the sound of a bum slamming into the side of the bum-mobile and exploding.

'Cover me!' said Eleanor, leaping onto the top of the bum-mobile. She knelt down, grabbed hold of the entry hatch and pulled it open.

But a bum was heading straight for her.

Zack heard it, spun around, took aim and fired.

It was a direct hit.

The bum released a volcanic geyser of brown liquid and then blew apart completely, covering both Zack and Eleanor with something very similar in consistency to chocolate mousse except much, much stinkier.

'I did it!' Zack said to Eleanor, jumping up and down. 'I did it!'

'That's great,' said Eleanor lowering herself down into the hatch. 'But what are you going to do about that?'

She pointed behind Zack and then disappeared into the bum-mobile.

Zack looked around.

What he saw made his stomach drop.

An enormous boulder was rolling down the hill towards them.

Only this was no ordinary boulder.

It was a bum-boulder.

Hundreds of bums clustered together. Hurtling across the grass. Crushing saplings like matchsticks.

Zack stared at it.

The bum-boulder was less than fifty metres away.

'Well don't just stand there, you idiot,' yelled Eleanor, poking her head back up through the hatch. 'Jump in!'

Zack took one last look at the boulder, turned and with an almost superhuman effort, jumped straight into the bum-mobile, pulling the hatch shut behind him.

Eleanor was in the front dome of the bum-mobile, strapping herself into one of the pilot seats.

'Hold on,' she yelled. 'Firing bum-thrusters.'

But before Zack had a chance to grab hold of anything the bum-mobile roared into life. Suddenly he was staggering backwards as they shot up into the sky.

Zack hit the back wall of the bum-mobile and fell sideways, his face pressed against the perspex dome. He saw the bum-boulder smash into the willow tree and burst apart, sending the bums flying into the air. They quickly regrouped and began chasing the bum-mobile.

'They're after us!' Zack yelled.

The bum-mobile suddenly dived.

This time Zack went flying forwards and fell heavily on the controls in the front dome, landing with his face pressed hard against the windscreen.

'You idiot!' screamed Eleanor. 'Why aren't you strapped in?'

'I didn't have time!' he said.

But Eleanor wasn't listening.

She was too busy concentrating on the huge mass of bums speeding towards them. There must have been at least five hundred of them. A big angry wasp-like cloud of bums.

'Uh-oh,' she said. 'Hold on, we're going to have to corkscrew.'

'What does that mean?' said Zack.

Eleanor pulled down hard on her steering wheel. The bum-mobile started looping in a series of smaller and smaller circles.

Zack had been feeling sick already, but this was the last straw.

He threw up. In a corkscrew pattern. All over the controls, the windscreen and the floor.

Eleanor was frantically trying to wipe a clean space on the windscreen to see through when Zack slipped and fell on top of her.

Eleanor's head hit the left side of the bum-mobile with a thump and she slumped in her chair, completely knocked out.

With nobody at the controls, the bum-mobile flipped upside down and Zack fell backwards and landed against the hatch with such force that it sprang open.

As Zack fell he grabbed the edge of the hatch and held on for his life.

Zack's heart was pounding as he took stock of his predicament.

He was hanging from an upside-down, out-of-control bum-mobile with a posse of angry bums hot on his tail. Within moments they were at his feet, and at the head of the pack were two bums that he recognised only too well.

'Greetings, my dear boy,' said the first bum. 'What a great pleasure to see you again. Don't you agree, Maurice?'

'Oh yes, your highness,' said Maurice smiling dourly. 'It is indeed a great, great pleasure.'

CHAPTER THREE

THE B-TEAM

The Prince and Maurice might have been glad to see Zack, but he certainly wasn't glad to see them.

As the Prince buzzed around him, Zack tried to kick his ugly little face, but he was too fast. All Zack succeeded in doing was kicking off the Prince's paper crown.

'Dear me,' the Prince said to Maurice. 'That's not a very nice greeting. And after all we've done for him.'

'Perhaps we should teach him some manners, sir?' said Maurice.

'An excellent idea,' said the Prince. 'After you, my dear Maurice.'

'That's very kind of you,' said Maurice. 'Very kind indeed. Very, very . . .'

'Maurice!' said the Prince.

Maurice sped up and launched himself into Zack's stomach. Zack gasped, completely winded. It felt to him like he'd just caught a medicine ball full in the guts. And before he could catch his breath, the Prince did the same and winded him again.

As they repositioned themselves for another attack, Zack put one arm in front of his stomach to protect himself. Maurice's next attack came not on Zack's stomach, however, but on his right hand: the hand he was using to grip the hatch.

Maurice came in hard and fast, over and over again, while the Prince continued to pound Zack's stomach and the bum-mobile plummeted ever faster towards the ground.

Zack tried to endure the pain, but he knew it wouldn't be long before his bruised fingers couldn't take any more.

And then he saw them. Three of the bravest and the best bum-fighters in the world were speeding up from the ground towards him on flying bums. The B-team!

Zack couldn't believe his luck. He had to blink a few times just to make sure he wasn't dreaming.

But it was them all right.

They were an amazing sight. Zack smiled. They were just like their pictures on the trading cards. And even though they were among the trading cards he'd swapped to get the Bum Hunter's card, he was still very pleased to see them.

Leading the charge was the Kicker, a large muscular man wearing a sleeveless black and white footy jumper and footy shorts. He had a big black bushy beard, thick black eyebrows and the most enormous feet that Zack had ever seen.

Right behind him was an equally huge woman who

was wearing an orange floral dress. She wore her hair in two enormous buns, one on either side of her head, and she had hands like baseball mitts. It wasn't hard to see why she was called the Smacker.

Bringing up the rear was a man dressed in a white three-piece suit. He had a white scarf around his neck and a red carnation in his left lapel. Apart from looking completely out of place riding on a bum, the other striking feature about him was his lips. They were big and red and wet-looking. He was known simply as the Kisser, and he was famous for his legendary 'kiss of death'.

The three riders whooshed up through the middle of the pack of bums, sending them flying in all directions.

The Kisser grabbed Zack around the waist and shot through the hatch with him. He brought the flying bum to a screeching stop, dismounted and ran to the front dome where Eleanor was hanging upside down in her seat, still unconscious.

The Kisser climbed into the seat beside her, strapped himself in and turned the bum-mobile 180 degrees. As he did so, Zack fell off the flying bum and crashed to the floor.

Right on top of the Kicker and the Smacker.

'Get off my head,' growled the Kicker.

'I'm sorry,' said Zack. 'It was an accident.'

'Accident my bum!' said the Kicker, picking himself up. 'I'm going to give your bum a kicking it will never forget. I'll teach you to be a bum sympathiser!'

Zack backed away from him. This strange, violent man was freaking him out.

'Now, now,' said the Smacker, stepping in between the Kicker and Zack. 'Nobody's going to kick anybody's bum until we know all the facts.'

'Kick first, ask questions later!' said the Kicker. 'That's my motto.'

Right at that moment a huge bum crashed into the roof. Another bum crashed into the floor. There was silence for a moment and then they heard a volley of bum-fire from the rear.

'No, Kicker,' said the Smacker, who quickly pulled the hatch shut. 'There's no time for that now. We've got a bum-blitz on our hands! They're coming at us from all directions!'

'Can't this thing go any faster?' bellowed the Kicker.

'I've got the gas on full already,' said the Kisser.

Zack glanced up towards the front of the bum-mobile and immediately wished he hadn't.

A big hairy bum had attached itself to the windscreen. Zack couldn't recall when he'd seen anything so horrible. It made him feel like throwing up all over again.

The Kicker shook his head in disgust.

'Leave it to me,' he said.

'No,' said the Smacker. 'Too dangerous.'

'Not as dangerous as flying with a big hairy bum on the windscreen,' he said.

He wrenched the hatch open, pulled himself up through it and dropped it shut.

The bum-blitz stopped instantly. Zack and the others watched the Kicker clomp along the roof to the front of the bum-mobile until their view of him was obscured by the hairy bum.

Suddenly the windscreen was clear, the hairy bum obviously booted to oblivion by the Kicker, who was standing on the nose of the bum-mobile, grinning widely and giving them the thumbs up.

Zack could see the other bums were keeping a safe distance, just out of kicking range. The Kicker turned towards them and beckoned them, daring them to come closer.

One did.

The Kicker booted it so hard that it split in two.

Another bum flew in from the left-hand side.

But the Kicker didn't even blink. He just lashed out with a perfect side-kick that sent the bum spinning.

The rest of the bums charged in fast after that, as if all keen to avenge the other bums. But if the Kicker was worried he sure didn't show it. He was drop-kicking and torpedo-punting and pirouetting—he looked amazing. Bums were flying everywhere.

'Look at him go!' yelled the Smacker. 'That's poetry that is!'

Zack wondered what sort of poetry described a brute in a footy jumper kicking bums senseless. Certainly not any of the poetry they gave him to read at school.

As Zack watched, he noticed that the Kisser didn't seem quite so enthusiastic about the Kicker's performance as the Smacker. He seemed to wince every time the Kicker's boot connected with a bum.

Meanwhile, one of the bums was orbiting the Kicker's head at high speed.

The Kicker was swatting at it with both hands like it was a particularly annoying mosquito, but the bum persisted, swatting clearly not being the Kicker's main strength.

All of a sudden the bum found the opening it was looking for and attached itself to the Kicker's face.

'Uh-oh,' said the Smacker. 'Looks like he's in trouble.'

The Kicker grabbed the bum by its cheeks and tried to pull it off, but it was too tightly attached. Meanwhile, the rest of the bums were coming in thick and fast.

'I've got to get out there!' said the Smacker, rising from her seat.

She pulled herself up through the hatch. Zack watched her stomp along the roof and out onto the nose of the bum-mobile. Then the action really started. He'd thought the Kicker was pretty spectacular, but the Smacker was something else again.

She rolled up her dress sleeves past her elbows, raised her enormous hands in the air and put on the most amazing display of slapping and smacking Zack had ever seen.

Backhanders, fronthanders, slaps, super-slaps, super double front and backhander power-slaps—there wasn't a smack or a slap that she didn't know. She smacked one bum so hard that it simply blew apart, smearing the windscreen with brown liquid.

'Damn,' muttered the Kisser, fumbling for the windscreen flusher.

When he'd got the window clean there was just the Smacker and the Kicker out on the nose alone. The Kicker still had the bum attached to his face, though, and the Smacker was holding him by the shoulder and smacking the bum with a front slap on one cheek and a backhander on the other.

After almost a minute of this punishment the bum fell off the Kicker's face.

The Kicker looked dazed and confused. He staggered backwards and Zack was sure that he was going to step off the nose of the bum-mobile until the Smacker grabbed him. She threw him over her shoulders in a fire-fighter's lift and walked back up the windscreen and across the roof.

Zack opened the hatch and the Smacker lowered the Kicker, still dazed, down into the bum-mobile.

He was in a bad way. His knees buckled and he sank to the floor. The Smacker lowered herself down next to him and closed the hatch behind her.

'I love the smell of freshly smacked bum in the morning!' she said. She went across to a small sink mounted on the wall of the bum-mobile and began to wash her hands.

'Call that smacking?' said Eleanor pulling herself up out of her seat.

'Eleanor!' said the Smacker, wiping her hands on the front of her dress. 'You're awake!'

The Smacker walked across to Eleanor and threw her enormous arms around her.

'It's good to see you,' said Eleanor after she emerged from the mighty hug. 'But why . . . how did you get here?'

'We saw your bum-mobile flying upside down. We caught this guy hanging from the hatch,' said the Smacker, pointing to Zack. 'We got here just in time.'

Eleanor glared at Zack.

'You idiot!' she said. 'You could have got us both killed!'

'It was an accident,' said Zack.

'You should have had your seatbelt on,' said Eleanor.

'I didn't get a chance,' said Zack. 'You went into that corkscrew thing and I've got a really weak stomach . . .'

'Don't remind me,' said Eleanor, screwing up her face.

'Aren't you going to introduce us to your boyfriend?' said the Smacker, grinning.

'His name is Zack,' said Eleanor. 'And he's *not* my boyfriend. I found him wandering the streets in the middle of a bum curfew. I saved his life. Biggest mistake I ever made.'

'Thanks a lot,' said Zack.

The Kicker groaned.

'Is he all right?' said Eleanor.

'He'll be fine,' said the Smacker.

'Ohhh,' he said, touching his nose. 'What happened? How did I get back here?'

'You got one on the face,' said the Smacker. 'How many times do I have to tell you—keep your head protected! Honestly, for an experienced bum-fighter you can be a real klutz!'

'I was doing all right,' said the Kicker.

'At getting yourself killed,' said the Smacker. 'Or at least rearranged.'

Zack felt a shiver run down his spine as he remembered what had happened to the bumcatcher at the rally.

'Excuse me,' he said. 'Did you say "rearranged"?'

'Yeah,' said the Smacker eyeing him suspiciously. 'What of it?'

Zack hesitated. 'Last night,' he said. 'I saw it . . . I saw someone get rearranged . . . it was horrible.'

'You saw a rearrangement?' said Eleanor, flashing an alarmed look at the Smacker.

Zack took a deep breath and told them the whole story.

When he'd finished Eleanor slammed her fist into the palm of her hand.

'I knew they were up to something,' she said, 'but I had no idea it was this big.'

'You think they're really capable of doing it?' said Zack.

'You'd better believe it,' said the Smacker. 'For the last thirty years we've travelled the world nipping bum uprisings in the bud wherever and whenever they appear. Most bum revolutions amount to little more than hot air—but it sounds like this one is more organised than most.'

'And Eleanor?' said Zack. 'Are you part of the B-team too?'

'Not exactly,' she said. 'But my father used to be, before he became a full-time Bum Hunter.'

'Your father's a Bum Hunter?' said Zack.

'Yes,' she said. 'His name is Silas Sterne.'

Zack gasped. He couldn't believe it. This was incredibly good luck. Silas Sterne was the one person who could stop his bum and save the world, and he was Eleanor's father!

'Where is he?' said Zack. 'Can you take me to him? We need to let him know what's happening.'

Eleanor shook her head.

'I don't know where he is,' she said. 'All I know is that I came home last week and he was gone. No note. Nothing. It's not like him at all.'

Zack gasped again. He couldn't believe it. This was incredibly bad luck. The one person who could stop his bum and save the world was missing.

'Do you have any idea where he went?' said the Smacker.

'Hunting the Great White Bum,' said Eleanor. 'Where else?'

The very mention of the Great White Bum sent new shivers down Zack's spine. The Great White Bum was in a class of its own. A rogue bum. Enormous. Evil.

There were many different theories about where it had come from. Some believed it to be a mutant bum created as an accidental side-effect of nuclear testing in the Pacific. Some believed it had been around for centuries. One Egyptian scholar had claimed to have discovered hieroglyphs depicting a large white bum. In his book *Chariots of the Bums* Eric Von Dunnycan even went so far as to claim that the Great White Bum was a space traveller who had arrived on Earth and taught ancient bums about bum liberation. Some believed it had been around for even longer than that: a sort of throwback to the age of the dinosaurs that had somehow avoided extinction—perhaps the first bum ever to grow legs and walk the face of the Earth.

'So what are we going to do?' said Zack.

'We've got to find that bumcano and plug it up as soon as possible,' said the Smacker. 'Let 'em stew in their own juices.'

'Give 'em a taste of their own medicine!' roared the Kicker, who had red cheeks now instead of the deathly white pallor of a few minutes before.

Eleanor nodded.

'I agree,' she said.

'Count me in,' said the Kisser.

'Me too,' said Zack.

'Uh-uh,' said Eleanor. 'Not you, Zack. We're dropping you off at the nearest bum shelter. This is a job for professionals.'

'But what about my bum?' said Zack.

'What about it?' she said.

'It's my bum,' said Zack. 'I want it back. I know it's a bit out of control right now, but I'm kind of attached to it.'

'Not any more you're not,' said Eleanor. 'What you need is a prosthetic bum.'

'A what?' said Zack, but Eleanor didn't answer him. Instead she turned around and flung open the lid of one of the padded bench seats that ran along each side of the bum-mobile. She rummaged around in the compartment underneath the seat and pulled out a bum. A clear wobbly silicon bum. She threw it to Zack.

'Here!' she said. 'Try this. It's a bit big but it'll do until you can get properly fitted.'

'But I don't want a false bum,' said Zack, throwing it down onto the floor of the bum-mobile. 'I want my real bum.'

'Don't be an idiot,' said Eleanor. 'Real bums are nothing but trouble. Sooner or later you're going to need to go to the toilet and I guarantee you, you're not going to care what sort of bum you've got.'

'She's right, you know,' said the Smacker, picking up the bum and gently putting it back in Zack's hands. 'We've all got falsies. They're the safest and the best. Take the bum. You'll need it.'

'I still think I should come with you,' said Zack.

'No, Zack,' said the Smacker. 'Eleanor's right about that too. A bumcano is no place for a civilian. For anyone for that matter. The odds are against us. But we've all had years of experience fighting bums. With a bit of luck we can tip the odds back in our favour. But not with you there, Zack. I'm sorry.'

'Perhaps you're right,' said Zack. He gripped the false bum and kneaded it back and forth in his hands. He knew that what Eleanor and the Smacker said made sense, but deep down he still felt responsible for all the trouble his bum had caused. It didn't feel right to just do nothing.

'Bum shelter ahead!' announced the Kisser. 'Beginning descent. Seatbelts on, everybody!'

The Kicker, Eleanor and Zack sat down and belted themselves in.

The bum-mobile dived at a steep angle. Zack could feel his ears popping. He could see through the front windscreen that they were heading towards an enormous stainless steel dome with the number '5' painted on the top. A little way to the left of it was a landing pad. Zack sat back in his seat and prepared for touchdown.

The Kicker was bending over, pulling his laces tight.

'Any bums try anything while we're down there and you know what I'll do?' he said.

'Kick their bums?' said Eleanor.

The Kicker guffawed and slapped her knee.

'You got it!' he said. Then, looking at Zack, his smile evaporating, he said: 'And if I see any bum sympathisers I'll kick their bums too.'

'I'm not a bum sympathiser,' said Zack, feeling scared again. The Kicker could kick bums, that was for sure—he just wished the Kicker would stop threatening to kick his.

'Bum-mobile BH-007 to Shelter 5,' said the Kisser into his handset. 'Permission to land requested. Over.'

The Kisser waited and then repeated his request.

'That's odd,' said the Kisser.

'What's the matter?' said the Smacker.

'I'm not getting any response,' said the Kisser. 'The radio is jammed. But there must be people inside the shelter. The brown flag is up.'

'Land anyway,' said the Smacker. 'We'd better check it out.'

'Roger,' said the Kisser.

There was a hissing sound and the bum-mobile began to descend.

The bum-mobile jolted to a stop.

'Uh-oh,' said the Smacker. 'Looks like we've got a welcoming committee.'

Zack looked out of the window. The bum-mobile was surrounded by a group of mean-looking bums armed with bum-trumpets.

'No wonder we've been having trouble getting through on the radio,' said Eleanor. 'They've been jamming it with high-frequency emissions. Leave them to me.'

Eleanor crossed the floor to a large black cabinet and opened it. Inside was the most amazing arsenal of bum-hunting weaponry Zack had ever seen. There was every sort of bum-fighting weapon imaginable: bum-guns, spear guns, harpoons, stun guns and long pointy sticks, some of the most deadly of all bum-fighting tools. There were bum-magnets, bum-shields, pink fluffy toilet seat covers, toilet brushes, soaps in plastic holders, clothespegs, rolls of sandpaper hanging on ready-to-roll dispensers and a full range of deodorisers and disinfectants.

Eleanor replaced her bumblaster in the rack and selected a smaller gun with a large round barrel. A Constipator 240. Zack recognised it as a clogger. He knew they were good for inhibiting enemy fire.

Eleanor clipped it to her belt, and pulled down something that looked like a leaf blower.

'That looks like a leaf blower,' said Zack.

'That's because it is,' said Eleanor. 'You can fight hundreds of bums at a time with a leaf blower. It's also good for cleaning up and clearing the air afterwards.'

Eleanor slung the leaf blower across her shoulder and draped a rack of rubber bum-plugs across her chest.

'Hold it,' said the Kisser. 'Let me handle this.'

Eleanor looked slightly disappointed.

'Are you sure?' she said.

'Yeah,' said the Kisser. 'No point in using up ammunition if it's not strictly necessary. Besides, I could do with the exercise.'

'Well, if you insist,' said Eleanor.

'Oh, but I do,' said the Kisser. He stood up, applied some fresh lip-gloss and brushed down his suit.

'Good luck,' said Zack.

'Never fear,' he said over his shoulder as he climbed out of the bum-mobile, 'the Kisser's here!'

Zack locked the hatch and then sat back down in the cockpit. He watched the Kisser approach the circle of bums.

They saw him and turned.

The Kisser bowed very low, so low his head almost touched the ground.

The bums moved in around him, but the Kisser made no attempt to escape. Instead, he did something very strange. He began to dance.

Zack watched with a mixture of confusion and amusement as the Kisser gyrated his hips and swayed from side to side in front of the bums. But as the Kisser danced, an even stranger thing began to happen. The bums, as if mesmerised, began to dance with him. They moved slowly from side to side, mimicking his movements with a sort of clumsy grace.

Then, without stopping his dance, the Kisser began motioning to one of the larger bums to come to him.

At first it seemed hesitant, but slowly, almost against its will, it crept forward until it was close enough for the Kisser to touch. The Kisser then reached out and tickled the bum under its arm.

As the Kisser tickled it, the bum seemed to undergo an amazing transformation. Its cheeks went bright pink. It blushed and went weak at the knees. At this point the Kisser reached out and picked it up with both hands—it offered no resistance—brought it to his lips and kissed it. The bum went limp, as if dead, or at least in a faint. The Kisser laid it on the ground next to him and began motioning to another bum, which submitted itself to him as easily as the first.

Having charmed the bums the Kisser was now disarming them as if they were no more dangerous than a pack of marauding marshmallows.

It didn't take long before he had kissed and immobilised every last bum. They lay in a large pile beside him.

'Wow,' said Zack. 'That's incredible!'

'Better him than me,' said the Kicker. 'There's no way I'd want to kiss a bum. Not in a million years.'

Zack watched the Kisser produce a silver hipflask from inside his jacket, tip his head back and swill the contents. Then he spat out a mouthful of greenish liquid and dabbed at the corners of his mouth with his white handkerchief. He took another swig and repeated the process.

'What's he doing?' said Zack.

'Gargling,' said the Smacker. 'I have to wash my hands after fighting bums, the Kicker has to polish his boots, and the Kisser has to wash his mouth out with industrial grade disinfectant. As the great bum-fighters have always said, if you want to make it as a bum-fighter, you have to keep it clean. It's a dirty business.'

Eleanor opened the hatch.

'Let's go,' she said, climbing out of the bum-mobile. The Kicker and the Smacker followed her.

Zack was about to follow them when the radio crackled into life.

'Bum shelter 5 to bum-mobile BH-007,' said a voice. 'Do you copy?'

Zack picked up the handset and pushed the button.

'Loud and clear,' he said.

The radio seemed to be working fine now that the bums were out of action and no longer able to jam the airwaves.

'What is your position, bum-mobile BH-007?' said the voice.

'We're on your landing pad,' said Zack.

The voice on the other end spluttered.

'You're what? You're in extreme danger! Repeat. Extreme danger. Do not leave your craft under any circumstances. The whole area surrounding the bum shelter is infested with bums!'

'It's okay,' said Zack. 'The B-team has them under control.'

'You're the B-team?' said the voice. '*The* B-team?'

'Well,' said Zack, 'I'm not. But the B-team is standing on your roof next to a pile of freshly kissed bums.'

'Unbelievable,' said the voice. 'We'll be right up.'

Zack climbed out of the cockpit, out through the hatch and jumped down onto the landing pad. He walked across to the pile of bums. 'Are they dead?' he said to the Kisser, who was applying fresh lip-gloss to his swollen lips.

'No,' said the Kisser. 'Just resting. They'll stay like that for a few weeks now. Plenty of time to be relocated to somewhere else where they can't do any harm.'

'Plenty of time to kick their bums, too,' said the Kicker surging forward.

'No,' said the Kisser, stepping between him and the bums. 'They're not hurting anybody. Leave them be.'

'But they're bums,' said the Kicker. 'Dirty, stinking, rotten, no-good, filthy, smelly bums!'

'Save your energy,' said the Smacker. 'You're going to need it. We've still got a long way to go.'

The Kicker looked at the Kisser.

'Whose side are you on anyway?' he snarled.

'Isn't that obvious?' said the Kisser, dabbing at the corners of his mouth with his handkerchief, which was not quite so white any more.

'Ignore him,' said the Smacker. 'He's spouting more hot air than all these bums put together.'

'Boy, are we glad to see you!' said a voice behind them. 'Those bums have been giving us merry hell all morning.'

Zack turned around to see a small officious-looking man. He was dressed like a soldier from the First World War.

'Welcome to Bum shelter 5,' he said, saluting. 'I'm Captain Vincent Brown. Won't you all come inside? It's crowded, but we've always got room for a few more.'

'Thanks,' said the Smacker. 'But we've got to keep moving.' She put her hands on Zack's shoulder. 'We just want to leave young Zack here, if that's okay with you.'

'That's fine, of course,' said the Captain. 'Any friend of the B-team is a friend of ours.'

Zack turned to the Smacker trying to blink back tears. 'I really wish I could come with you,' he said.

The Smacker put her arm around him.

'You have to stay, Zack,' she said. 'You don't want to get mixed up with the world of bum-fighting.'

'I'm already mixed up in it,' he said. 'That's my bum out there. I've got a responsibility to stop it. If anyone can talk it out of this, I can.'

'No, Zack,' said the Smacker gently. 'You've got a false bum now. Put it on and forget about your first one. Here, I'll give you a hand. Just loosen your belt a little.'

Zack was too upset to argue. He loosened his belt. The Smacker took the false bum from Zack's hands and pushed it down the back of his pants and into place.

She patted it gently.

'How's that?' she said.

Suddenly Zack was overwhelmed by a powerful urge to go to the toilet.

'Where's the nearest toilet?' he asked Captain Brown.

'Just go down the steps and turn right,' he said.

Zack made it just in time. He was pleased to discover that the false bum worked just like a regular bum. In fact in at least one way it was even better—it was self-wiping.

Maybe the Smacker was right, thought Zack. He

wondered if he'd be better off staying at the bum shelter with his false bum and forgetting about his real bum.

But he couldn't.

His bum was trying to take over the world.

He couldn't just stay there and pretend it wasn't happening.

He had to do something.

He knew that the B-team weren't going to allow him to come with them. Not if they knew about it. But what if they didn't know about it? What if he stowed away?

Zack figured that all he'd have to do is to stay hidden until they'd passed out of the range of any other bum shelters and then they'd have no choice but to take him.

It was worth a try.

Zack climbed back up the steps to the door.

At the top of the steps there was an emergency telephone.

He wondered whether he should ring his gran and let her know that he was all right. If his plan to stow-away worked he might not get another chance and there was no telling how long he would be away. He didn't know what he would tell her, but he didn't want her to be worrying about him. She had enough to worry about, what with the war and probably her own bum before too long.

Zack rang her number.

She picked up the receiver after only one ring, as if expecting his call.

'Hello?' she said. 'Zack? Is that you?'

'Yes, Gran,' said Zack, a bit surprised. 'How did you know?'

'You weren't in your bed this morning. Is everything all right?'

'Sure, Gran,' said Zack. 'I'm fine.'

'Really?' said his gran. 'I thought you might have been conscripted . . .'

Suddenly Zack had his excuse. It was perfect.

'Actually,' he said, 'I *have* been conscripted. I might not be home for a while.'

'Do you know where they're sending you?' she said.

'I'm on a secret mission, Gran . . .' he lied. 'Can't say too much on the phone . . .'

'I quite understand,' she said.

'Thanks, Gran,' said Zack. 'I've got to go now.'

'Well, good luck,' she said. 'I've just got one piece of advice for you, Zack.'

'What's that, Gran?' he said.

'Don't forget to wash your hands!'

And then she was cut off.

Zack tried to ring back, but the line was dead. Why had Gran warned him to wash his hands? he wondered. It was a strange piece of advice to give somebody who was apparently going off to war. Unless it was a *bum* war, of course. But how could she have known that? It was probably just a grandmotherly sort of thing to say, like 'Look both ways before you cross the road', or 'Remember to brush your teeth'.

Zack shook his head. Whatever it was he didn't have time to figure it out now. He had to get on board the bum-mobile while there was still time.

CHAPTER FOUR

NED SMELLY

The B-team was still where Zack had left them, deep in conversation with Captain Brown.

And even better still, they had their backs towards him.

But he knew he had to be quick.

Zack ran across the roof of the bum shelter and leapt onto the landing pad. He ran to the far side and hid behind one of the wheels of the bum-mobile.

So far so good.

Now he just had to work out where to hide.

There was no room inside the bum-mobile. It would have to be the cargo hold. He grabbed the handle of the heavy metal door and pulled as hard as he could.

The door opened easily and there would have been plenty of room except that there were two large metal drums taking up most of the space.

Zack grabbed one of the drums. He expected it to be too heavy to move but he had to try. To his surprise it shifted easily. It was completely empty. So was the other one.

Zack lifted both the drums out and hid them behind a small shed at the back of the launching pad.

There was not a moment to spare.

Captain Brown, Eleanor and the B-team started walking across to the landing pad. They were talking about how to dispose of the kissed bums.

'Don't touch them for a few days,' said the Kisser. 'Leave them until they've degassed themselves. They'll be less dangerous to move.'

Zack dived into the cargo hold and pulled the door shut behind him.

It was cold and there was a ridge of metal sticking into his back, but even though he was uncomfortable, Zack knew he was doing the right thing.

He heard footsteps approaching the bum-mobile.

'Zack's taking a long time,' said Eleanor.

'Probably still a bit upset that he couldn't come with us,' said the Smacker. 'We might have to leave without saying goodbye.'

'Don't worry,' said Captain Brown. 'I'll see that he's taken care of.'

'Thanks,' said the Smacker. 'Tell him we're sorry we had to go, but that there wasn't a moment to lose.'

'Will do,' said the Captain. 'Good luck!'

'Good luck nothin'!' said the Kicker. 'I'll kick their bums so hard they'll wish they never had them.'

'But they *are* bums,' said Eleanor. 'How can a bum not have a bum? It would just be a hole.'

'Then I'd kick that as well,' said the Kicker.

Zack heard them climb inside the bum-mobile.

'Prepare for take-off,' said Eleanor.

The bum-mobile roared into life. Zack felt it rise slowly through the air and then Eleanor fired the thrusters and the bum-mobile took off.

The thrusters were near the cargo hold and Zack could feel the heat through the floor. It was radiating up through his fake bum. He hoped that fake bums were fireproof as well as self-wiping.

But despite being cramped and having a hot bum, Zack was warm and sleepy. He closed his eyes.

He wasn't sure how much longer it was until he opened them again, but he knew he'd had a good sleep.

He could hear shouting.

'. . . we should kick their bums!' ranted the Kicker. 'It's the only way!'

'Now listen up,' said the Smacker. 'This is no ordinary mission. We could be in for the fight of our lives. Our success is going to depend on us working as a team, not just going in kicking and smacking and kissing and shooting. We're going to need to work smarter than that.'

'And *then* we'll kick their bums!' said the Kicker.

Zack heard the Smacker sigh.

'Yes,' she agreed, as if talking to a child, 'then we'll kick their bums.'

'I've got the bumcano on the radar,' said Eleanor. 'It's incredible—I've never seen so much bum activity concentrated in the one spot. And there are bums pouring in from all directions.'

'How far away is it?' said the Kisser.

'I'd say about six hours flying,' said Eleanor. 'We have to cross the Great Windy Desert.'

'What's the pong factor outside?' said the Smacker.

'Extreme,' said Eleanor. 'We must be approaching the desert now.'

The bum-mobile lurched sideways.

Zack started to feel sick again.

'Uh-oh,' said Eleanor. 'Hold onto your hats. There's a lot of wind out there.'

An alarm sounded. The bum-mobile started to shake as it went into a series of violent dips and climbs.

'Oh no!' said Eleanor. 'We're out of gas! Just what we needed.'

'Have you got reserve tanks?' said the Smacker.

'Yeah,' said Eleanor. 'There are two cans in the cargo hold.'

A fresh wave of nausea flooded through Zack. But this wasn't anything to do with the movement of the bum-mobile. This was to do with the two cans he'd removed from the cargo hold.

He didn't feel any better, either, when he realised that what he thought was the wall between him and the cabin of the bum-mobile was actually a sliding door.

Zack tried to roll as far back as possible, but it was too late. The door slid open, light flooded in and he saw the Smacker staring at him.

'Zack?' she said, frowning. 'What on Earth are you doing in there?'

Zack just looked at her.

He couldn't bring himself to tell her what he'd done.

He didn't have to.

'There are supposed to be two spare gas tanks in here,' she said. 'You took them out to make room for yourself didn't you?'

'I thought they were empty,' he said. 'They were so light . . .'

'Bum-mobile gas is lighter than air,' said the Smacker, flexing her enormous hands, which Zack was scared she would soon be using on him.

'Have you found them?' called Eleanor. 'I can't hold it much longer.'

'All I've got is a stowaway,' said the Smacker, yanking Zack out of the hold.

'What?' said Eleanor, glancing around. 'Zack? But what . . . why . . . where are the fuel tanks?'

'He removed them,' said the Smacker.

'I told you he was a bum sympathiser!' roared the Kicker. 'He's on their side! He's sabotaged us! I'm going to kick your . . .'

Suddenly the bum-mobile lurched sideways and went into a nose dive.

'We're going to crash!' yelled Eleanor. 'Brace yourselves!'

Eleanor and the Kisser curled over in the crash position.

The Kicker and the Smacker both grabbed handholds and pushed their backs against the bum-mobile wall.

Zack sat down, put his arms over his head and waited for the crash.

He didn't have to wait long.

WHAM!

The bum-mobile hit the ground. Zack was thrown forward towards the hatch. He put his hands out in front of him. The hatch opened. He went flying out and landed head-first in an enormous clump of thistles.

But they weren't like normal thistles. They seemed to be made of stainless steel—and they stank.

Luckily the needle-like thorns had missed Zack's eyes, but he felt like they were stuck in every other part of his body.

But even worse was the terrible smell. It was hot and a strong wind was blowing.

What next? thought Zack. As if having his bum trying to take over the world wasn't bad enough, now he'd caused the B-team to crash their bum-mobile.

For all he knew they could all be dead. And as usual, it was all his fault.

Then he heard Eleanor.

'Zack, you idiot!' she yelled. 'I'm going to kill you!'

'Can you get me out of these thistles first?' he asked.

He felt Eleanor's hand around his ankle and with one hard yank she pulled him free.

'Aaaggghhh!' screamed Zack, as hundreds of needles were pulled from his flesh at the same time. 'Easy does it!'

'Easy does it nothing!' said Eleanor. 'You're in big trouble!'

Zack was lying on his back on hot sand, looking up at Eleanor's face as if in a nightmare. Her eyes were bugged out and she appeared to be frothing at the mouth. Above her the sky was a bright brilliant blue. And the wind roared around them, blowing sand into Zack's ears, eyes and mouth.

'You idiot!' she screamed. 'You absolute idiot! You idiotic stupid moronic bloody idiotic idiot!'

'But . . .' said Zack.

'Don't interrupt me,' spat Eleanor. 'I haven't finished yet, you crazy lame-brained pathetic dumb klutz fool!'

'You forgot "idiot",' said Zack.

But Eleanor's only response was to put her hands around Zack's throat and start squeezing as hard as she could.

'No, Eleanor!' he yelled, but all that came out was a high-pitched strangled noise.

In the distance Zack could see the bum-mobile stuck nose-first in the sand. It was planted almost vertically. But apart from the bum-mobile there was nothing. Just desert as far as he could see. Hot windy stinky desert broken only by the occasional clump of the needle thistles. It was very much what Zack imagined Hell would be like, except without the flames.

'I really don't think you should do that,' said a voice. 'You might hurt him.'

'That's exactly what I intend to do!' said Eleanor.

'No,' said the voice, 'I think that's a bad idea. Life is hard enough out here.'

'You got any better ideas?' said Eleanor.

'Yes,' said the voice. 'Let him go. And have some of this oxygen. I think you're suffering from methane madness.'

Zack felt Eleanor's hands release their grip on his throat.

Zack looked up and saw a strange-looking man. He looked like a desert island castaway. He had a long beard and was wearing frayed and torn pants cut off at the knees. His skin was burnt a deep reddish-brown colour by the intense sun. But the really strange thing about him was that he was wearing scuba-diving gear—twin oxygen tanks on his back, a mouthpiece and a face mask.

He took the mouthpiece out of his mouth and gave it to Eleanor. She gulped deeply.

'Hey, not too fast,' he said. 'Just take it slowly.'

Once she was calm, he knelt down next to Zack, who was still coughing and choking.

'Here,' he said, offering Zack the mouthpiece. 'Take some of this. The methane in the desert wind is pretty poisonous. It does strange things to your head. Breathe it for too long and it will kill you.'

Zack took some deep lungfuls of oxygen.

It felt wonderful.

After a couple of minutes the man pulled the mouthpiece back out of Zack's hands and took a few breaths for himself.

Suddenly Eleanor jumped up, screaming and slapping at her legs.

'What's the matter?' said the man.

'There's something in my pants!'

'Don't worry,' he said. 'It's probably just stinkants. They won't hurt you. Try not to squash them though.'

'Why not?' said Eleanor, still hopping and slapping.

'Because if they pop, they stink,' said the man matter-of-factly.

Eleanor immediately stopped her mad dance, and stood there squirming instead.

'So what do I do?' she said.

'Just stand still,' said the man.

He pulled a small cloth bag from the pocket of his shorts, opened the neck and poured some small white crystals around her feet.

'What is it?' said Eleanor.

'Needleweed sugar,' he said. 'It's very sweet. They love it.'

Zack watched, amazed, as a line of fiery red ants appeared at the bottom of Eleanor's trouser legs, marched across her foot and swarmed all over the sugar.

'Amazing things, stinkants,' said the man. 'They're the only things that can survive out here—except for me and the needleweeds.'

Zack winced. He already knew about needleweeds.

'You live out here?' said Eleanor, staring at the man as if he was completely mad.

'Yes,' he said. 'The Great Windy Desert is where the old farts come to die—including me!'

He laughed in a wheezy high-pitched way, which degenerated into a coughing fit. He took a few mouthfuls of his oxygen.

He held out his hand.

'My name is Ned,' he said. 'Ned Smelly.'

'Ned Smelly?' said Eleanor. 'Didn't you used to be a Bum Hunter?'

He nodded slowly.

'How did you know that?'

'I've heard my father talk about you.'

'Your father is a Bum Hunter?' he said. 'What is his name?'

'Silas Sterne,' said Eleanor.

'Ahh! Silas!' he said. 'The greatest of the greats! We hunted together on many occasions. In fact, he was with me on my last hunt—the hunt that earned me my name. You see, I haven't always been called Ned Smelly. But after our run-in with Stenchgantor, the Great Unwiped Bum, I was never the same.'

'What happened?' said Zack.

'Well,' said Ned, 'to cut a long story short, I copped a full blast from the beast. To this day I haven't been able to get rid of the stench. That's why I live out here on the edge of the Great Windy Desert. My body odour is too offensive for normal human company.'

'I can't smell anything,' said Zack.

'Oh yeah?' said Ned, raising his arm up and exposing his armpit.

Zack wasn't even close, but it was the worst thing he had ever smelt.

The smell was so bad he started clawing at his nose to try to rip it off his face.

'Hey, steady on,' said Ned, offering Zack his oxygen mouthpiece. 'Have some of this.'

Zack breathed it in and calmed down.

'Thanks,' he said. 'I needed that.'

'Your father, as usual, came away from the encounter unscathed,' said Ned. 'But Stenchgantor remains, to this day, living in the Brown Forest.'

'I thought it was the *Black* Forest,' said Zack.

'Not any more,' said Ned. 'Not since Stenchgantor took up residence there.'

Ned turned to Eleanor.

'Is there anyone else in the bum-mobile?'

'Oh no!' said Eleanor. 'The B-team! I completely forgot about them. Come on!'

Ned and Eleanor ran to the bum-mobile. Zack followed them, but he couldn't run. His feet were still full of needleweeds.

By the time Zack got there, Ned and Eleanor had pulled the Kicker, the Smacker and the Kisser out of the bum-mobile and laid them in the shade of one of its wings.

They were all unconscious, but Ned used his oxygen tank to revive them and pretty soon they were all coughing and spluttering and the Kicker was threatening to kick Zack's bum again.

After thinking that he might have killed them all, Zack felt relieved and almost happy to hear the Kicker's threat again. In fact, he almost would have been glad if the Kicker had followed through. Zack knew he deserved it.

'What brings you out here anyway?' said Ned, passing the Smacker his mouthpiece.

The Smacker explained the situation.

'That would explain all the flying bums I've been

seeing lately,' said Ned. 'Thousands of them. All flying north. Big packs. There goes one now.'

They all looked up into the dazzlingly blue sky and saw a squadron of bums flying in a large bum-shaped formation, sounding like a squadron of bombers.

'Wow,' said the Kisser. 'What a sight! There must be at least ten thousand of them up there.'

'Wish my legs were longer,' said the Kicker. 'I could give 'em what's coming to 'em right now.'

The bums moved surprisingly fast across the sky. The group watched them until they disappeared into the horizon.

'Why is the sky so blue here?' said Zack.

'It's the methane,' said Ned. 'It intensifies all the colours. But it also makes you go a bit crazy.'

'Everybody knows that,' said Eleanor, looking at Zack pointedly.

Zack shrugged and looked at the ground.

'Go easy on Zack,' said the Smacker. 'We've all got to learn sometime and I reckon Zack's been on a pretty steep learning curve in the last twenty-four hours.'

'Yeah,' said Eleanor. 'Now he knows all about why it's a dumb idea to remove the spare gas cans from a bum-mobile.'

'I oughta kick your bum,' said the Kicker, staring at Zack with his unblinking red eyes, his face impassive and his voice low and dangerous.

'Here, have some oxygen, you two,' said Ned, rushing across with the mouthpiece. 'You're getting overheated.'

As Eleanor and the Kicker gulped their oxygen, Ned turned to the Smacker.

'I've got to get you all inside,' said Ned. 'Methane madness will send you all insane. Why don't you come back to my shack? It's air-conditioned. Rest. Have a meal.'

'Impossible,' said the Smacker. 'We haven't got time. We have to get to the bumcano before it's too late.'

'And how exactly do you plan to do that?' said Ned. 'You won't be going anywhere in that bum-mobile in a hurry.'

Zack could see that he was right. The bum-mobile was a mess.

'Do you know where we can get another bum-mobile?' said the Smacker.

Ned shook his head.

'The only bum-mobiles around here are the ones that crash. I keep a shed full of spare parts. I trade them occasionally for oxygen tanks. I may be able to fix yours.'

'How long would it take?' said the Smacker.

'Hard to say,' said Ned. 'One, maybe two weeks. Perhaps a month.'

'We haven't got that much time!' said the Smacker, jumping up and grabbing Ned by the collar. 'Don't you see? It could be all over by then. A world controlled by bums. IS THAT WHAT YOU WANT???'

She was screaming and shaking Ned by the throat.

'Help!' gasped Ned. 'Oxygen!'

Zack grabbed the tank off Eleanor, rushed it to Ned and offered him the mouthpiece.

'Not me,' said Ned, pushing it towards the Smacker, 'her!'

Zack pushed the mouthpiece into the Smacker's mouth.

She breathed deeply. Her arms relaxed. Ned removed her hands from around his throat.

'I'm sorry,' said the Smacker. 'I don't know what came over me.'

'It's all right,' said Ned. 'The effects of methane madness are nothing new to me. It can really do strange things to your head. I spent the first six months of my time here in a methane delirium. I thought I was the king of a large country and all the stinkants were my subjects. That was until I was able to build a shack and rig up a basic air-filtering system and calm myself down.'

Zack wasn't sure that Ned wasn't still in some sort of delirium. After all, he lived in the Great Windy Desert—one of the vilest places on Earth as far as Zack could see. And smell.

'The truth of the matter,' said Ned, 'is that you can't make it without a bum-mobile.'

'We'll go by foot,' said the Smacker.

'Are you kidding?' said Ned. 'Look, I've been to this vol . . . I mean *bum*cano.'

'You have?' said Eleanor.

'Yes,' said Ned. 'I went there with your father once. It's located on a small island in the middle of the Sea of Bums. Heard of it?'

'Of course,' said Eleanor. 'The sea contains some of the oldest bums in the world.'

'And some of the most dangerous,' said Ned. 'Bums with teeth. Bums with electrical charges. Huge stinging bumrays that span twenty metres and . . .'

'Are you trying to scare us?' said the Smacker.

'I'm just trying to make you see reason,' said Ned.

'He said, "I'd better dig in quick",' said the Smacker, seizing the serving forks and putting a small amount on the Kicker's plate. 'Because it looks so delicious it might not last long.'

'Oh, no need to worry about that,' said Ned. 'There's no shortage. This is the Great Windy Desert, you know. If we run out I can easily scare up some more.'

The Smacker served the Kicker, ladled out a tiny amount for herself, and then pushed the bowl across the table to the Kisser and Eleanor whose faces were both white.

'After you,' said the Kisser to Eleanor, pushing the bowl towards her.

'No, after you,' said Eleanor, pushing it back.

'No, no, no,' said the Kisser. 'Ladies first. I insist.'

'You're too kind,' said Eleanor, her eyes narrowed.

'Don't mention it,' said the Kisser.

'Oh, but you are,' said Eleanor, taking the serving forks. 'The least I could do is to serve you first.'

And with that Eleanor began piling the Kisser's plate high with the evil-smelling concoction.

'That's enough,' said the Kisser. 'No more, I beg you!'

'Don't be silly. You haven't even got any stinkants yet,' said Eleanor, upending most of the bowl onto his plate.

'Yep,' said Ned, who was shovelling his food into his mouth at an incredible rate. 'Great source of protein! What about you, Zack? Not eating?'

Zack was trying to think of an excuse for not eating when Eleanor grabbed his plate.

'I was just about to serve him,' she said.

'No, that's quite all right!' said Zack, trying to grab his plate back. But Eleanor was too quick. She piled what remained of the needleweeds onto his plate along with what was left of the stinkants.

'There you go,' she said, flashing Zack the fakest sweet smile he'd ever seen. 'Eat it all up now. There's a good boy.'

'Thanks,' he said. 'But what about you? Don't you want some too?'

'I'd love to,' she said. 'But I'm on a diet. I can eat pretty much anything I want except for stinkants and needleweeds. It's a pity—they look delicious.'

'I've got some spurts in the cupboard,' said Ned. 'Left over from the last plague. They're a bit dry, but quite edible.'

'No, it's okay thanks,' said Eleanor quickly. 'Besides, I'd better get our gear ready. We've got a long trek ahead of us and we want to get as far as we can before sunset.'

'Okay,' said Ned, picking up his plate and licking it clean. 'I'll come and prepare your oxygen tanks.'

Zack sat there and stared at the big green pile in front of him. The Kicker was right. Dog sick would be better than this. He picked up a forkful of the seaweed-like needleweeds and put them in his mouth. He tried to chew it but felt the urge to vomit again.

'Excuse me, Ned,' said Zack. 'Which way to the bathroom?'

'End of the corridor,' he said.

Zack ran. He went in, shut the door and knelt down in front of the toilet bowl, but away from the smell of dinner and the stench of Ned he felt instantly better.

He looked around the bathroom. Like the rest of the house, it had been put together from the remains of bum-mobiles. There was a forty-four gallon drum which had been cut in half to form a bath, and a sheet of stainless steel attached to the bathroom wall to serve as a mirror. Beside it was a large cabinet. It looked like the cabinet that housed the bum-gun arsenal in Eleanor's bum-mobile.

Zack pulled it open, curious to see if Ned kept the same array of weapons, but what he saw was unexpected.

There was every type of soap, perfume and BO spray you could imagine. Cakes of soap stacked high, liquid soap dispensers, roll-on deodorants, stick deodorants, spray deodorants, at least fifty different bottles of perfume, mouthwash and aftershave, as well as thirty different brands of toothpaste.

Poor Ned, thought Zack. He'd salvaged and presumably used all these products and yet he still smelt terrible. And here he was trying to look after them and all they could do in return was be rude about his food.

Zack went back to the table. The others had left. Their plates were still full of food. Zack grabbed a spoon and started to eat. He didn't stop until he'd eaten everything on his plate. Then he ate everybody else's servings as well.

After Zack had finished he went outside to Ned's shed where the others were getting suited up. Ned's shed resembled a wrecker's warehouse—stocked with every conceivable bum-mobile spare part and accessory. Ned had obviously been collecting bum-mobile debris for a long time.

'Hey!' said the Kicker, pointing to a panel of the wall made from the front section of a bum-mobile and with 306-BF painted on the side. 'Didn't that belong to the F-team?'

'I think you're right,' said the Smacker, strapping an oxygen tank onto her back, and going over to examine the panel more carefully. 'How long ago did you find this, Ned?'

Ned looked up from the belt he was adjusting for Eleanor while she stood there pinching her nose.

'Hmmm,' he said. 'About four years ago. Found it in the great basin valley about an hour north of here.'

'Four years ago!' said the Kicker. 'That's when they disappeared. So that's what happened to them. Were there any survivors?'

'None,' said Ned. 'By the time I found them they were just bleached bones in the sand. The stinkants had stripped them clean.'

'I thought you said stinkants were harmless,' said Eleanor.

'Mostly,' said Ned. 'The ones around here are. But the further you get into the desert the larger and more aggressive they become.'

Eleanor made a face and Ned went back to adjusting her tank.

'Any stinkants come near me and \ bums!' growled the Kicker.

'How can you kick an ant's bum?' said \ 'Wouldn't it be too small?'

'No bum is too small for me to kick,' said the K\

'Why not just step on them?' said the Kisser.

'Because I like kicking!' said the Kicker. 'Got a problem with that?'

'No problem at all,' said the Kisser. 'I just sometimes wonder if kicking is the best answer to everything.'

'What's wrong with you?' said the Kicker. 'You're talking like a bum sympathiser. And you know what I do to bum sympathisers?'

'Yes,' sighed the Kisser. 'I think I can guess.'

'Yeah?' spluttered the Kicker, scraping the ground with his foot like a bull about to charge. 'Well guess this!'

'Oxygen, Kicker!' commanded Ned.

The Kicker took the mouthpiece and took a deep breath.

'I want you all to take oxygen at least five times an hour,' said Ned. 'Any more and you'll risk running out before you've crossed the desert. Any less and you risk methane madness. Any questions?'

'What about when we're asleep?' said Zack.

'Nobody will be going to sleep,' said Eleanor. 'If you want your beauty sleep then you'd better stay here.'

Zack looked at the Smacker. She nodded.

'Eleanor's right, Zack,' she said. 'Think you can handle the pace?'

'Sure I can,' he lied.

The truth was that he didn't know if he could handle the pace. He'd never done a non-stop three-day trek through a desert full of methane and flesh-eating stinkants before. But he was determined to find his bum and get to it before it did anything really insane or before the Kicker kicked it to pieces. And as much as he liked Ned, he wasn't keen to spend a moment's more time at his shack than he had to.

Eleanor pushed a pack into Zack's hand.

'Here's your rations,' she said. She gave packs to everybody else. 'I've put in as much food and water as the packs will hold. Go easy on it because I'm not sure how long we'll have to hold out.'

Zack pushed his breathing tank to the side and put the pack on. The supplies were heavy, but he figured it beat eating needleweeds and stinkants.

'Ned,' said Eleanor, patting a pile of boxes. 'These provisions are for you. We can't carry them so you might as well have them.'

Ned's eyes filled with tears.

He seemed to be overwhelmed by Eleanor's generosity.

'Thank you,' he said, reaching out to hug Eleanor, who took two quick steps backward. 'Thank you all very much. I only wish you could stay longer. It's been good having your company.'

'We'll call in on the way back,' said the Smacker.

'I'll have a meal of needleweeds and stinkants waiting for you,' said Ned.

The group trudged out of Ned's shed and into the desert.

The sky seemed bluer than before, and the sand

even more yellow and the heat and the wind even more intense.

They each pulled on the diving masks Ned had given them, took a deep breath of oxygen and waved goodbye to Ned.

'Good luck!' said Ned, standing in the doorway of his shack. 'God knows you're going to need it!'

'We're going to kick their bums!' yelled the Kicker above the roar of the wind.

CHAPTER FIVE

METHANE MADNESS

The wind roared.

Zack trudged, sometimes sinking down to his knees in the loose sand.

He fought his way out.

He sucked on his oxygen.

He trudged.

The wind roared.

It was hard work. And not just for Zack.

After about ten minutes the Kisser called for a rest.

'I have to go back,' he said. 'I left my lip-gloss behind.'

'Can't you pick it up on the way back?' said Eleanor.

'No,' said the Kisser. 'Without my lip-gloss I run the risk of my lips cracking, and without my lips I'm completely powerless.'

'All right,' said the Smacker. 'Go back and get it.

We'll wait, but hurry up. We've already lost a lot of time.'

The Kisser nodded and turned back.

Eleanor and the Smacker were clearly annoyed by the interruption, but Zack was glad of the rest. He sat back on his pack and took a deep gulp of oxygen. Then he took a deep gulp of water. Then another gulp of oxygen.

'Go steady on that,' said the Smacker. 'Remember what Ned said. Don't use it all up now.'

'Yeah, I know,' said Zack. 'It's just that the air is so thin. I can hardly breathe.'

'I knew we shouldn't have let him come,' said Eleanor. 'He got us into this mess in the first place and all he's doing now is complaining about it.'

'Calm down,' said the Smacker. 'The only person who's holding us up at the moment is the Kisser and he's had more experience than most of us.'

Eleanor snorted.

Zack lay back on his pack, closed his eyes and tried to imagine he was anywhere else but the Great Windy Desert. He thought about swimming at his local swimming pool. With his real bum on. The water was wet. Cool. And there was lots of shade.

He was woken up by a sharp pain in his arm. He opened his eyes. The Kicker was standing there, about to kick him again.

'Wake up!' he said. 'We're moving!'

Zack got up. The Kisser was back. He was standing there applying lip-gloss with the tip of his finger, very gently and delicately, and even though he was wearing a three-piece suit he seemed to have hardly broken a sweat. Even the carnation in his lapel looked fresh.

They began marching again. Eleanor was out front, followed by the Smacker. The Kisser was in the middle. Zack was behind him but was having trouble keeping up because his stomach was aching. The pain had started soon after they'd left Ned's place and had gradually become worse. He wondered if it had been such a great idea to eat so many needleweeds and stinkants.

Behind Zack was the Kicker who, true to his name, gave Zack a kick in his false bum every time he slowed down.

'Cut it out will you?' said Zack, after one particularly violent kick.

'Keep up with everyone else,' said the Kicker, 'and I won't have to kick you.'

The Kisser turned around.

'Lay off him, Kicker,' he said. 'He's just a kid.'

'He's still got to keep up with everybody else,' grumbled the Kicker.

'Let me put it this way,' said the Kisser. 'Kick him again and I will kiss you.'

'If you so much as lay a lip on me I'll kick your bum,' growled the Kicker.

'Oxygen, you two!' said the Smacker.

They obediently took their oxygen as the Smacker commanded, and the group resumed trudging. With one difference. The Kicker stopped kicking Zack.

They trudged.

The wind roared.

They sucked their oxygen, drank their water, ate

their anti-bum energy bars and kept trudging through the harsh flat desert, the horizon broken only by the ugly jagged clumps of needleweeds.

They trudged till the sun went down, till the moon came up, till the moon went down and the sun came up again.

There was little talk. They were too tired to talk. They only had the energy to trudge.

The sun was high in the blue sky when they came across the wreck of the bum-mobile that the Kicker had recognised as belonging to the F-team. Much of its shell was submerged in sand. The Kicker stopped and started digging. He pulled out a long white bone and studied it.

He shook his head.

'They were a good team,' he said. 'Saved my life once. Pity I'm too late to return the favour.'

He lay the bone carefully back into the sand and covered it. Zack watched a single tear creep from the edge of the Kicker's eye, run down his cheek and make a small dark circle on top of the little mound of sand.

The group resumed trudging, not wanting to stand in the one place for too long as the stinkants would cover their boots within moments.

Zack checked his oxygen supply gauge. It was low. He wondered whether he'd end up like the F-team, just a pile of bones in the sand.

They had been trekking up a sand hill for what felt like forever to Zack when he drank the last mouthful of water from his canteen. Knowing that he had no more water seemed to make him thirstier than ever. He couldn't stand it. All he could think about was water.

'I'd give anything for a glass of water!' he said. 'A big cool glass of water—big enough to swim in!'

'I could go a pint of beer,' said the Kicker.

'I'd settle for the barmaid's lips,' said the Kisser, applying more lip-gloss. 'Just a pair of soft red lips . . .'

'You know what I'd kill for?' said the Smacker. 'A massage. That's all I want. I'm aching all over. Eleanor—what'll you have?'

'An ice cream,' said Eleanor dreamily. 'A double-header dairy queen with nuts and sprinkles and chocolate coating . . . mmm . . .'

As she said this they reached the top of the dune.

Zack couldn't believe what he saw. None of them could.

There, spread out below them was a vast blue lake of crystal clear sparkling water. Around its edges were palm trees with big shady branches.

'Wow,' said Zack. 'An oasis!'

'That's funny,' said the Smacker, frowning. 'Ned didn't say anything about an oasis.'

'That's probably because he's never made it this far before,' said the Kicker.

'Last one in is a rotten bum,' said Eleanor, taking off down the hill towards the lake.

Zack threw his pack off and chased after her.

He heard the Smacker calling them back, but there

was no way Zack was going back. He wanted that water.

Zack turned around and beckoned to the Smacker, Kicker and Kisser to join him. He saw the B-team shrug and start to run after them. Zack grinned, turned and kept running.

But Eleanor was unbeatable with her head start. She threw off her pack and oxygen tank and weapons as she ran and dived in fully clothed. Zack made a close second. He was followed by the Kisser and the Kicker who both hit the water at the same time, creating a massive splash.

The Smacker was last, but not least, creating the biggest splash of all.

Zack treaded water, every pore of his skin drinking in the wetness. After more than thirty-six hours in the Great Windy Desert the cool water was just what he needed.

Eleanor splashed a handful of water at him.

Zack splashed back. She laughed. It was the first time Zack had seen her laugh since he'd met her. He had to admit to himself that she looked pretty. Especially as she wasn't frowning and calling him an idiot.

Suddenly the Kicker started yelling.

'Look!' he cried. 'A bar!'

Zack looked. Sure enough, there was a small hut with a thatched roof. At the front was a friendly-looking barmaid leaning on a counter. Behind her were shelves lined with bottles.

'And a barmaid!' yelled the Kisser. 'With lips!'

She waved at them.

'And an ice cream van!' said Eleanor.

That was funny, thought Zack. He hadn't noticed it before, but parked right beside the tropical bar was a colourful ice cream van, playing a distorted rendition of 'Greensleaves'.

'A massage table!' said the Smacker. 'And a masseur! What are we all waiting for?' she yelled. 'Let's go!'

They ran out of the water and up the beach to the bar and the ice cream van and the masseur.

Zack looked around him in wonder—all thoughts of psycho bums and bum-hunting and Great Windy Deserts completely out of his mind.

Eleanor came towards him holding two double-decker dairy queen cones. She handed him one. He took it, licked the top and then bit into the cold creamy centre. It was heaven.

The Kicker was leaning against the bar, his head back, tipping the last of his pint into his throat. He slammed the glass down on the counter beside him, burped, and wiped the back of his hand across his mouth.

'I'll have another!' he said loudly, but the barmaid was not listening to him. She was too busy giggling and flirting with the Kisser—so the Kicker reached over, grabbed the tap and filled the glass up himself.

Meanwhile the Smacker was lying on the massage table, her face a mixture of something like pleasure and pain as the muscle-bound masseur chopped and smacked and pummelled her body, paying particular attention to her meaty hands.

Zack turned to Eleanor. They raised their ice creams

and 'cheers'ed' each other. It was all so perfect, so beautiful. Zack felt it had been worth every painful moment of the last thirty-six hours.

He took another bite of his ice cream. But something was wrong. It wasn't soft and sweet like before. It was hard and gritty and tasted like . . . stinkants!

Zack looked at the cone. It was covered in stinkants. So was his hand . . . and his arm . . . his whole body was covered with stinkants. Biting and burning and eating him alive!

He looked around. The lake had disappeared. So had the bar and the ice cream van and the masseur.

They were all lying in the sand, covered in stinkants!

Everybody started screaming. They jumped up and brushed wildly at the ants. They were all doing the same mad wild dance, the ants biting and popping and stinking in equal measure.

Zack realised that none of what they had just experienced was real.

It was all madness.

Methane madness.

And judging by what they could see on the horizon, it wasn't over yet.

The biggest, dirtiest, blackest most terrifying tornado was twisting towards them—snaking and whipping at high speed with a terrifying roar.

'Stink tornado!' yelled the Smacker. 'Run!'

But no-one needed to be told to run, least of all Zack.

He was already running.

As fast as he could.

But it wasn't easy running across the sand. It was more like wading than running.

He was wading in slow motion, still trying to brush the stinkants off his arms, his face, out of his eyes, ears and nose.

All the while the roar of the tornado was getting louder and louder behind him.

The sky was no longer blue—it was a deep purple—the air thick with sand.

'We're not going to make it!' yelled the Kisser. 'We're doomed!'

As far as Zack could tell the Kisser was right.

There was nowhere they could run to get away from the tornado.

Zack dropped to his knees, flattened himself against the sand and prayed for the tornado to pass over him.

He felt a sharp pain in his ribs.

He looked up.

It was the Kisser, staggering around, blinded by the sand, his hands desperately clawing the air in front of him.

'Get down!' yelled Zack.

But the Kisser obviously couldn't hear him above the deadly roar of the tornado.

Zack pushed himself up, grabbed the Kisser's hand and tried to pull him down, but it was impossible. The Kisser's body was floating in the air above him, as if he was a helium balloon that Zack had just won at the show. Then he was sucked up into the tornado—and Zack with him.

It was the wildest, craziest merry-go-round of Zack's life. He was being spun around as if he were no heavier than a piece of confetti, rising higher and higher all the time. The air around him flashed red and silver with stinkants and needleweeds. He saw other objects too. The shell of an old bum-mobile. A bleached human skull. A gigantic stinkant. Zack held onto the Kisser as if his life depended on it which it did.

Suddenly Eleanor floated in front of his face.

With his free hand Zack grabbed her hair. Eleanor grabbed his arm.

'We need to swim to the middle!' yelled Eleanor. 'To the eye of the tornado. It will be safer there. We can drop straight to the ground!'

She started kicking her legs and holding her free arm out like an aeroplane.

Zack motioned to the Kisser to do the same.

The Kisser, though clearly terrified, nodded and started flapping his arm and kicking.

The closer they got to the centre, the faster they seemed to be moving. Zack was finding it difficult to see clearly. But there was no mistaking the Smacker and the Kicker as they floated into view, holding onto each other.

The Smacker reached out and grabbed Eleanor's hand and with the extra weight they were able to make faster progress towards the centre of the tornado.

All of a sudden the roaring stopped.

There was no sound at all.

Zack realised they were dropping down through the eye of the tornado at high speed.

The ground was coming up fast.

'What do we do now?' he yelled to the Smacker.

'Hope for the best,' she said.

'Okay,' said Zack.

He closed his eyes. It felt like the G-forces were sucking his face off.

Zack screamed and blacked out.

When he came to, his face was resting on something soft. Smelly and soft.

It looked like mud.

It smelt like mud.

It tasted like mud.

It *was* mud.

Zack lifted his head up, spat, wiped his cheek and looked around.

He was in a forest. Everything was wet and muddy. And brown. The mud, the trees—even the sky—all brown.

Like most places he'd visited in the past twenty-four hours, it stunk. But the stink was slightly different. It was more the smell of rotting wood, of decay, of dank mud.

In the distance Zack could hear voices.

He picked himself out of the mud and pushed through some densely packed trees, the ground sucking at his feet as if reluctant to let them go.

From the edge of a small clearing Zack could see four figures—each as brown as the forest. One of them waved at him.

'Zack!' called the Smacker. 'Over here!'

Zack walked across to them, squelching up to his ankles in mud.

'Welcome to the Brown Forest,' said the Smacker.
Zack gasped.

The Brown Forest.

He remembered that Ned Smelly had mentioned the Brown Forest. He also remembered that Ned had mentioned that Stenchgantor, the Great Unwiped Bum, lived in the Brown Forest. And that was one bum Zack did not want to meet.

Stenchgantor was listed in the *Bumper Book of Bums* as the stinkiest bum in the world. Most bums only registered one or two points on the Rectum scale, but Stenchgantor came in at a nose-bruising 9.8 points, which made him even stinkier than the Great White Bum, although nowhere near as intelligent.

'We've got to get out of here,' said Zack. 'Stenchgantor could find us!'

'Don't worry,' said the Smacker. 'He's not anywhere around here.'

'How do you know?' said Zack.

'We'd smell him,' said the Smacker.

'But it smells pretty bad already,' said Zack.

'I know,' said the Smacker, 'but believe me, Stenchgantor smells a lot worse.'

'I say we catch some bums, saddle them up and have a look around,' said the Kicker.

It was the first time Zack had heard the Kicker mention bums without threatening to kick them.

'And how do we do that?' said Eleanor. 'We've lost everything we had in the tornado. We don't have any bait. We don't even have a fluffy pink toilet seat cover.'

'I do,' said Zack. He pulled the seat cover out of his utility belt.

'How about this?' he said, handing it to Eleanor.

She eyed it critically. 'Bit worn out, but it will do,' she said.

Zack noticed that despite the fun they'd had in the methane delirium, Eleanor was obviously still in no mood to forgive him.

'This might be a dumb question,' said Zack, 'but how is a fluffy pink toilet seat cover going to help us?'

'Bums love fluffy pink toilet seat covers,' explained the Kisser. 'In fact, they are powerless to resist them. Place a fluffy pink toilet seat cover out in the open and the bums will come. You can be sure of that. Then it's just a simple matter of catching them, corking them and sitting on top.'

'I don't suppose you've got a net as well?' said Eleanor.

'As a matter of fact,' said Zack, 'I do.'

He pulled a small net out of the belt. Zack had to admire the bumcatcher. He'd thought of everything. Zack gave the net to Eleanor.

She examined it.

'Hmmm,' she said. 'Not bad. Bit on the small side, but it'll have to do I suppose.'

The Kisser took the pink fluffy toilet seat cover from Eleanor. 'Watch this,' he said to Zack.

He walked to the middle of the clearing, placed it on the ground, and then returned to the others who were hiding behind a large mouldy tree stump.

'Give them a few minutes,' he said. 'Eleanor, you ready with the net?'

'Ready,' said Eleanor, crouching into a sprint position.

They didn't have to wait long.

The first bum to arrive was a small pink one with a large pimple on its left cheek. Zack watched it fly down out of the sky and alight about a metre from the seat cover. The bum took a few cautious steps towards it and then stopped, looking around as if suspecting a trap. Then, having satisfied itself that all was in order, the bum leapt into the middle of the seat cover, wriggling with contentment in the fluffy pink fur.

'Now!' whispered the Kisser.

Eleanor shot out and threw the net over it. The bum didn't even try to get away. It just seemed to nestle deeper into the seat cover. Eleanor brought it back and handed it to Zack.

'That can be yours,' said Eleanor. 'It's small and won't have too much power.'

'Thanks,' said Zack, holding the wriggling and squirming bum as far away from himself as possible. When bums were frightened there was no telling what they were capable of doing.

'Here, give him to me,' said the Kisser.

Zack was more than happy to get rid of the bum.

As he did so, two more bums arrived. They were chunky, muscle-bound bums and immediately began fighting over the seat cover. The slightly larger one sat on it, but then the second bum picked it up and hurled it clean across the clearing, and took its place on the cover. But the first bum wasn't about to be beaten that easily. It came running back across the clearing and kicked the other bum through the air.

'All right!' said the Kicker under his breath.

Zack was both amused and shocked. He'd always thought that bums fought humans—not other bums.

But the bum that had been kicked was not about to give up. It returned and they ended up grabbing each other like a pair of sumo wrestlers—the seat cover in between them.

'Better stop them before they exhaust themselves,' said the Kisser.

Eleanor nodded and walked quietly forward and, despite her claim that the net was too small, brought it down easily over the pair. They struggled and fought to get out of the net until the Kisser poked his finger through the hole and tickled them, which instantly seemed to calm them down.

The final two bums also appeared together—a pair of Siberian Screaming Bums. They created such an awful ear-piercing noise when captured that Zack had to stick his fingers in his ears. The Smacker had to put both of the bums over her knee and smack them for a full five minutes before they shut up.

The five bums were all assembled on the ground and corked by the Kisser, with corks from the bum-catcher's belt.

'Now watch closely,' said the Smacker. 'This is how to make what we call a bum-hopper. The average bum has enough gas to propel itself and a rider for about twenty minutes. But you don't let it out all at once.'

'Why not?' said Zack.

'You've seen a balloon when you blow it up and let it go without tying the end?' she said, making a loud raspberry noise and waving her hand around in the air.

Zack grinned and nodded.

'Well,' said the Smacker, 'that's why you just let out a little at a time. Like this.' She pulled the cork out slightly on one of the screaming bums. Only a fraction of the screaming noise escaped. 'Just that much would be enough to send you over half a kilometre,' she said. 'It's more like leapfrogging. Let a bit out, rise, fall, land, rise and so on. Stops you going too high, too fast.'

'How do I steer?' said Zack.

The Smacker frowned. 'Normally we have bridles, but we haven't got any at the moment, so we're just going to have to pinch them. Pinch on the right and it will veer to the left to try to get away from the pain. Pinch the left cheek and you'll go right. Two pinches on either side will make you turn even sharper. Got that? The main thing to remember, though, is not to leave the cork out for too long.'

Zack didn't know any more about flying bums than he did about flying bum-mobiles. But it seemed straightforward enough. Pinch right to go left. Pinch left to go right. Don't let too much gas out. What could be so hard about that?

'All right, team,' said the Smacker once they were all mounted on their bums. 'We're going to try and bum-hop our way to the coast. We don't know how far away we are, so we may need to stop and capture new bums. Keep together, watch out for low branches, and watch out for bum bogs!'

And saying that, the Smacker reached behind, lightly tapped her cork and immediately took off through the trees.

The Kicker was next, riding one of the screamers, and Eleanor followed him on the other.

'You next,' said the Kisser. 'Bum voyage!'

Zack reached around, pulled the cork out slightly and took off into the trees with a whoosh.

Before Zack knew it he was heading straight towards a very thick tree trunk. He pinched the left side of his bum-hopper's cheek to go right, but he pinched it on the pimple by mistake.

The bum flinched and let out a rush of gas.

The bum-hopper veered right. But too far right!

He pinched the right side once more.

It veered left. But too far left!

He pinched the left side again, and accidentally pinched the pimple again.

The bum flinched and shuddered, and let out another burst of gas—this one even bigger than the first.

Zack went to jam the cork back in, but the cork was missing.

The bum-hopper was swerving left, right, up and down. It was completely out of control. Zack didn't know whether he was heading north, south, east or west. In fact, it felt like he was travelling in all four directions at once.

Zack gave up pinching and just hung on for his life.

The bum-hopper whooshed through the trees faster and faster until he could hardly breathe and then WHAM! Zack crashed into a branch. The bum shot out from under him. Zack grabbed frantically at the branch and held on for a moment, but it was covered in slippery brown moss and he fell, straight into a big soft pool of brown mud.

Or at least he thought it was mud.
But it wasn't.
It was bog.
A bum bog.
And Zack was in it right up to his neck.

CHAPTER SIX

STENCHGANTOR

Zack tried to swim towards the edge of the thick brown bog, but it was no use.

He could feel the bog sucking and pulling him down.

Eleanor was right, he thought. He should have taken her advice and stayed in the bum shelter. He could have been happy with his false bum. After all, it was self-wiping. And what more could anybody ask of a bum?

Zack was getting tired. The midnight bum rally, the bum-mobile crash, the Great Windy Desert, methane madness, the stink tornado, the Brown Forest and now this. They had all taken their toll. And to make things worse he hadn't had a proper meal since the needleweeds and stinkants, not that he felt like eating anything with his churning stomach. All he wanted to do was sleep. His arms and legs were moving more and more slowly as he felt the tiredness spread through his body—his mouth sinking closer and closer to the bog as he closed his eyes and began to nod off.

But just as the bog was about to pull him under, Zack heard someone call his name.

'Zack? Zack, are you there?'

Zack opened his eyes as wide as he could and tried to focus on the voice, which seemed to be moving through the trees towards him.

'I'm here!' he called.

Then, as if in a dream, Zack saw Eleanor riding towards him on her bum-hopper.

She dismounted and stood at the edge of the bog.

'Don't tell me,' she said. 'It was an accident.'

Zack nodded.

'You have a lot of those, don't you?' she said.

'How did you know I was here?' said Zack, ignoring her jibe.

'I didn't,' said Eleanor. 'The Kicker said you sped past him on an out-of-control bum-hopper. If it had been up to me I wouldn't have wasted time looking for you. But the Kicker insisted.'

That was the nice thing about Eleanor, thought Zack. She didn't leave you guessing about how she felt about you. She just came right out and told you.

'Thanks for your honesty,' said Zack, shrugging off the tiredness. 'Now, can you help me get out of here?'

'I don't know,' she said. 'You're a long way out and a long way under, but if I hover over the top of you I might be able to pull you out.'

She got back on her bum-hopper and floated out over the top of the bog.

'Give me your hand,' she said, reaching down.

Zack strained to pull his arm free of the sucking bog and reached out to grab Eleanor's hand. But she was too far away.

'I can't reach you,' he yelled. 'Can you come any lower?'

'I'll try,' she said.

She lowered her bum-hopper as close as she could, her knees almost touching the bog.

Again she stretched out her hand.

Zack touched her fingertips, but still couldn't get a grip.

'Closer!' he yelled through the gritty bog that was seeping into his mouth.

Eleanor leaned right down, her knees bent and feet tucked up. This time she grabbed Zack's hand and started to pull.

KERSPLUDGE!

Suddenly Eleanor was in the bog beside Zack, up to her neck as well. And she wasn't happy.

'You idiot!' she said.

'It wasn't my fault!' said Zack.

'You're still an idiot!' she said, trying to swim for the edge of the bog, but getting nowhere.

'You're the idiot,' said Zack, who was sick of being blamed for everything that went wrong. 'You can't even keep your balance on a bum-hopper.'

Eleanor's face contorted with rage.

'Right, you!' she said, throwing a big handful of bog in Zack's face. A bit splashed onto her bum-hopper. It took fright and shot off into the forest.

'If that's how you want it, then fine!' yelled Zack

and he heaved a big bogload back at Eleanor. It hit her right in the mouth.

'You've had that coming for a long time,' he said.

Eleanor's only reply was a double-handed bog-lob, which somehow, to Zack's surprise, managed to hit him in both ears at the same time.

He was about to retaliate but stopped when he noticed Eleanor's face. She had her head cocked to one side, listening intently.

'Do you hear that?' she said.

'What?' said Zack.

'That crashing,' she said. 'You can feel it.'

She was right. It was impossible to tell what direction it was coming from, but the bog was vibrating all around them.

Then the smell hit.

A smell like no other.

'Are you thinking what I'm thinking?' said Zack.

'I think I am,' said Eleanor. 'If he finds us here we're dead.'

'We're dead anyway,' said Zack. 'If he doesn't find us we're going to drown in this stink bog.'

The pounding was getting louder.

That's when Zack felt a rumble. Just small at first, but it was definitely a rumble. Zack felt it deep inside him. He recognised it as the sort of rumble that usually came after he'd eaten too many baked beans. But he hadn't eaten any baked beans. Just needleweeds and stinkants.

'Uh-oh,' said Zack.

He knew what was coming next. He felt another rumble, even deeper this time.

'Grab my hand!' he said to Eleanor.

'Why?' said Eleanor.

'Just do it!' he said.

Zack felt the most extraordinary force moving through his stomach and out through his false bum. It was volcanic in its intensity. He felt like a NASA space shuttle breaking free of its launch tower and heading up into the sky.

SQUELLLLLLLLLLLLLCH!

Zack and Eleanor's bodies left the bog.

They rocketed up through the trees.

Zack looked at Eleanor.

She was grinning from ear to ear.

'Enjoying the ride?' he said.

She nodded.

'I can't believe it,' she said. 'For once you've done something right!'

Zack couldn't believe it either.

It seemed too good to be true.

It was.

Zack began to realise they were heading too high. Too fast. He had no idea how powerful needleweeds and stinkants really were. And he'd eaten everyone's share as well as his own.

They arced over the tops of the trees and started their descent.

Fortunately it was into an area where there weren't so many trees.

Unfortunately, there was a reason for that. They were heading straight for the lair of Stenchgantor.

There was no mistaking him.

Below them was the ugliest, dirtiest, wartiest, pimpliest, grossest, greasiest, hairiest, stinkiest, most unwiped bum Zack had ever seen.

But as ugly as Stenchgantor was, the worst thing about him was definitely his stench: a foul nauseating stink that made Zack not only want to rip his nose off but also plug up his ears, eyes, mouth and every single pore of his skin as protection against its corrosive blast. It was definitely not a smell that crept up on you—it was a smell that walked right up and punched you in the face—and then kept on punching, each punch harder than the last.

'Help!' screamed Eleanor, letting go of Zack's hand.

Zack knew he had really done it this time.

His only consolation was that he figured the situation couldn't get any worse.

And then it did.

Stenchgantor turned around and looked up at them.

Zack stared back.

As long as he lived he would never forget the horror—the horror of that enormous single unwiped eye staring up at him.

Not that he had very long to look at it.

Zack and Eleanor whooshed past the enormous brown vortex and bounced hard against the chunky outgrowths of Stenchgantor's rubbery bottom. Eleanor hit one cheek and Zack hit the other. But although the cheek broke Zack's fall, it had a trampoline effect and sent him flying back in the direction he'd come. Unfortunately the same thing had happened to Eleanor, and she was flying straight back, too, on a collision course with Zack.

They clonked heads midair and plummeted to the ground—Zack landing on top of Eleanor, right in between Stenchgantor's legs.

'Sorry,' he said to Eleanor as he rolled off her. She didn't respond. With a sinking feeling he realised he'd knocked her unconscious again.

But that was the least of his problems.

Zack looked up.

Stenchgantor was even more terrifying from this angle.

Twenty metres of the sheerest, ugliest bum imaginable.

Well, unimaginable really.

And unwatchable.

Zack's eyes were watering and burning from the stench.

Zack wiped them, but they immediately filled up with tears again. It was like peeling onions. But worse.

Stenchgantor stamped his feet and seemed to laugh. The ground shook and clouds of choking gas billowed out and enveloped Zack and Eleanor.

Zack looked down and noticed the muddy floor of the forest was littered with bones.

Human bones.

They obviously weren't the first visitors to Stenchgantor's lair. Zack realised this must be where everyone lost in the Brown Forest eventually ended up.

Zack shook Eleanor's shoulder.

'Wake up!' he said. 'We're going to have to make a run for it!'

Eleanor didn't move.

Zack was searching his belt for something to revive her when Stenchgantor spoke in a deep booming voice: 'Fee Fi Fo Fum—I smell the smell of two false bums!'

Stenchgantor bent down towards Zack and Eleanor and stared at them with his terrifying brown eye.

Or was it an eye? wondered Zack. Stenchgantor had just said that he could *smell* their false bums. Perhaps the eye was a nostril, he thought. But that was impossible. Bums didn't have nostrils. That was the source of their power. Unlike humans, they were completely unaffected and unhampered by a sense of smell.

Unless Stenchgantor was somehow different . . .

Zack waved his arms.

Stenchgantor didn't react.

He's blind! thought Zack.

Perhaps that was the clue to defeating him.

Stenchgantor had to be powerful enough to withstand his own stench—that was obvious—but could his sense of smell make him vulnerable to a stench greater than his own?

No, of course not, Zack told himself. That was ridiculous.

Zack wondered if his brain was being affected by methane madness again.

Even if Stenchgantor could be defeated by a stench

greater than his own, what could possibly have a greater stench than Stenchgantor?

And then the bumcatcher's voice came into Zack's head. Loud and clear: *'The socks, Zack, remember the socks . . .'*

Zack remembered putting on the socks the bumcatcher had given him and how he had worried they would make his foot odour worse. *But perhaps that was the point!*

Stenchgantor bent down over Zack and Eleanor and sniffed with his huge brown nostril.

It was now or never.

Zack reached down, pulled off his shoes and peeled one of his socks off.

'Pwoarrr!' said Eleanor, coughing and choking herself back to consciousness. 'What's happening? Where are we? And what's that awful stink?'

'It's Stenchgantor!' yelled Zack.

'No I mean that *really* awful stink,' said Eleanor.

'That would be my socks,' said Zack.

'Boy, you've got a problem,' said Eleanor.

'Let's hope Stenchgantor agrees with you,' said Zack, waving the sock in front of the Great Unwiped Bum.

But Stenchgantor continued to draw ever closer to them. From this close up his warts and pimples looked like enormous mountains. One pimple, a huge swollen red volcano, with what looked like at least three tonnes of custard in the top, looked ready to erupt as it came closer and closer to them.

'It's not working,' said Zack. 'Run for it!'

His socks were bad, but not bad enough.

Zack and Eleanor got to their feet and started to run but then Stenchgantor's voice boomed once again.

'FEE, FI, FO, FUM.

You cannot hide.

You cannot run.'

Once more the noxious stench enveloped Zack and his eyes began to water so much that he couldn't see where he was going.

He tripped and fell.

He wiped his eyes. A whole human skeleton lay on the ground in front of him, its hands around its throat as if it had died choking. Zack knew exactly how it felt. But he wasn't ready to join it. Not yet.

He took off his other sock.

A new wave of moist pungent putridity assailed Zack's nostrils.

His socks weren't helping. He'd only made things worse. As usual. Eleanor was going to kill him. If the smell didn't kill both of them first.

But then a strange thing happened.

As the fog slowly cleared Zack saw Stenchgantor coming towards them, but he wasn't running. He was staggering.

He seemed dazed and confused.

Then Stenchgantor's knees folded underneath him and he crashed to the ground, falling forward. Zack got up.

'Watch out!' he said to Eleanor, who was on her hands and knees a little way ahead of him, coughing and gagging.

'What?' she said.

Zack rushed forward, grabbed her hair and pulled her as hard as he could.

Luckily the ground was soft and slippery and it was easy to drag her.

'Ouch!' she yelled.

KERTHUMP!

Stenchgantor's body came to rest in the mud, right where Eleanor's body had been moments before.

Eleanor and Zack looked at Stenchgantor in awe. Zack had never seen a bum like him.

'Not bad,' said Eleanor, rubbing her head and nodding her approval of Zack's quick thinking.

'Reckon he's dead or just knocked out?' said Zack, still too shaken to realise that Eleanor had given him the closest thing yet to a compliment.

'Who cares?' said Eleanor. 'Let's just get out of here. We've got to try and catch up with the others before they reach the coast.'

'How?'

'Have you still got your fluffy pink toilet seat cover?' she said.

'Nah,' said Zack. 'The Kisser kept it.'

'Damn,' said Eleanor.

Overhead there was a droning sound. They looked up. A large squadron of bums was flying north. Zack and Eleanor watched them until they were obscured by the enormous pimple on Stenchgantor's hide.

Suddenly Eleanor punched Zack's arm.

'I've got it!' said Eleanor. 'I know how we can do it!'

'How?' said Zack.

'See that pimple up there?' she said. 'The one that looks like a mountain?'

'Yes,' said Zack. 'It's horrible. What about it?'

'Well, firstly,' said Eleanor, 'it's pointing in the same direction as the bums just flew in isn't it? Chances are they're heading for the bumcano. The coast must be in that direction.'

'Yes,' said Zack slowly, starting to see what she was getting at but, at the same time, not wanting to see.

'And, secondly,' she continued, 'the pimple is ripe for popping. All we have to do is to be on top of it when it blows and we'll hitch a ride to the coast. What do you think?'

'It's a terrible idea!' said Zack. 'I don't want to be covered in pimple pus. Especially not Stenchgantor's pimple pus!'

'You'd rather be rearranged by your bum?' said Eleanor.

'No,' said Zack, 'but . . .'

'But nothing,' said Eleanor. 'That's your choice. What's it going to be, Zack? Would you rather get a little pus on your pants or have a bum for a brain?'

Zack bit his lip and thought about it. As far as he was concerned it wasn't much of a choice.

'Zack!' said Eleanor impatiently.

'Okay,' said Zack. 'Pus it is.'

'Spoken like a true bum-fighter,' she said. 'Give me a boost up.'

Zack's head was swimming. But not because of the thought that he might soon be hurtling though the air covered in Stenchgantor's pimple pus. It was because Eleanor had said he had spoken like a 'true bum-fighter'.

He was no bum-fighter. He knew that. Sure, he'd wiped out Stenchgantor, but it was just a fluke. A lucky break. And the socks were the bumcatcher's idea in the first place.

Eleanor was wrong.

He wasn't a bum-fighter. And yet Eleanor's words filled Zack with a feeling of excitement like he'd never felt before.

Zack bent his knees, cupped his hands and pushed Eleanor up to a ledge created by a large cavernous dimple.

'Okay,' said Eleanor, offering Zack her hand. 'Your turn.'

He grabbed hold of her hand and she pulled him up. The ledge, like the rest of Stenchgantor, was soft and spongy.

Zack followed Eleanor's lead in using one of the hairs protruding from a wart to swing himself up to the base of the pimple.

The pimple rose smooth and tall into the air like a giant red lava lamp. Zack could see the blood and juices and big round globules of pus that had broken away from the motherlode at the pimple's summit—all percolating inside the jelly-like exterior that bore a spooky resemblance to a giant cow's teat.

'Okay,' said Eleanor. 'Now be very careful. We don't want to puncture it before we get to the top, otherwise it won't propel us anywhere.'

'But how can we possibly make it to the top?' said Zack. 'There are no footholds or handholds at all.'

He looked down into the water.

There were hundreds of tiny bums swimming around his legs. He had never seen bums swimming before.

Then the Smacker cupped her hands around her mouth, and Zack heard her loud and clear.

'Get out of the water!' she called. 'It's full of bum-piranhas!'

Zack stared dumbly at the bum-piranhas, too scared to move.

'Swim, you idiot!' yelled Eleanor.

Zack didn't need any more encouragement. He started thrashing his way to shore.

Normally Zack was not the world's fastest swimmer but he felt like he must have broken all known speed records getting out of that water. Not that he had time to celebrate the fact.

As soon as he hit the shore he jumped out and started hopping and kicking like a maniac, trying to get rid of a bum-piranha that had attached itself to his big toe.

The B-team came running down the sand towards him.

'Hold still!' yelled the Smacker. 'I'll smack it!'

'I'll kick its bum!' said the Kicker.

'No! Let me kiss it!' said the Kisser.

But Zack ignored all of them. He gave an enormous kick. The bum went flying off his toe and into Eleanor's head as she emerged from the water.

'Hey!' she said, gasping. 'Watch where you're kicking those things!'

The bum-piranha flipped around on the sand, its tiny jaws clapping like a pair of maracas.

The Kisser walked over, expertly picked it up between his thumb and forefinger and held it up for everyone to see. Zack looked closely—it was just like a normal bum except instead of legs it had fins.

'Fascinating little creatures, aren't they?' said the Kisser.

'That's one word for them,' said Zack shuddering.

The Kisser smiled and threw the little bum back into the water. For a few moments it just floated on the surface, as if stunned, then it seemed to come to its senses and swam away.

Zack breathed a big sigh of relief.

He thought that if he never saw another bum-piranha in his life it wouldn't be too soon.

'We looked everywhere for you,' said the Smacker. 'Where have you been?'

'Fighting Stenchgantor,' said Eleanor.

The Kisser gasped.

'Stenchgantor?' said the Kicker, looking surprised. 'But nobody's ever fought Stenchgantor and survived!'

'We did,' said Eleanor, patting Zack on his shoulder. 'Zack out-stenched him. He used his socks.'

The group all looked at Zack in amazement.

'I have very smelly feet,' explained Zack.

The group now all stared at Zack's feet in amazement.

'But you're not wearing any socks,' said the Smacker.

Now it was Zack's turn to look down at his feet in amazement. She was right. His socks were missing!

'Oh no!' he said. 'The bum-piranhas have eaten my socks! I've lost my most powerful weapon!'

The Smacker smiled. 'No you haven't,' she said, tapping the side of her head. 'A bum-fighter's most powerful weapon is in here. Don't underestimate yourself. You have talent.'

Zack's head was spinning.

First Eleanor had told him he'd spoken like a bum-fighter. Now the Smacker was telling him he had talent. But they were wrong. They had to be. He didn't have an ounce of bum-fighting talent in him. That's what the instructor at the Junior Bum-fighters' League had told him after he'd failed the entry exam for the third time. 'Face it, son,' the instructor had said, 'when it comes to bum-fighting you're a born spectator.'

Sure, Zack thought, he'd brought down Stench-gantor, but that was just luck. Beginner's luck.

'The raft is ready!' yelled the Kicker.

Zack looked at the bums that the B-team had lined up on the sand.

The bums were in ten rows, and in each row there were twenty bums. Zack wondered why they weren't all trying to run away but looking closer he could see that they were all lashed together with brown vines and fastened to eleven long pieces of bumboo. Like the bums used to make the bum-hoppers, they had all been corked.

'Come on,' said the Smacker. 'We have to hurry. The bums are getting more powerful every minute. We have to get to the bumcano before it erupts.'

As she spoke, a huge squadron of bums zoomed overhead in the direction of the bumcano.

Zack, Eleanor and the Smacker walked down and joined the group.

'Well?' said the Kicker. 'What do you think? Two hundred bum-power and completely unsinkable.'

Zack was impressed, but wasn't sure how the raft was going to be powered. He couldn't see any oars or paddles. He didn't want to say anything, though, in case it made him look dumb.

'Great work,' said the Kisser, kneeling down to pat one of the bums. 'How long do you think it will take to reach the bumcano?'

'Without a map it's hard to say,' said the Kicker. 'But with a bit of luck and a fair wind we should be there by nightfall.'

He slapped one of the bums as he said 'fair wind' and suddenly Zack understood how the bum-raft was going to work.

The Kicker and the Kisser dragged the raft down to the edge of the water. The bum-piranhas were waiting in the shallows.

'But what about the bum-piranhas?' Zack said. 'They're still there. Won't they eat the raft?'

'Funny thing about bums,' said the Smacker. 'They never eat their own kind. As long as you stay on the raft you'll be fine.'

'And if they try anything I'll kick their bums!' said the Kicker.

He pushed the raft into the water.

'Eleanor,' said the Kicker, 'you first, then Zack.'

Eleanor stepped on and went to the far end. Zack stepped on. The raft wobbled violently and Zack would have fallen off, but Eleanor reached out and steadied him.

'Thanks,' he said.

'Don't mention it,' said Eleanor. 'I owe you one.'

'Uncork the rear row!' said the Kicker, who was manning the rudder, which was made out of a thick slab of bum-tree bark.

Zack turned and watched as the Smacker and the Kisser knelt and pulled the corks out of the bums in the back row of the raft.

The effect was impressive. It was like having ten outboard motors all running at full throttle. The front of the raft rose into the air as the bums at the back roared into action.

'How long do the bums last?' Zack asked the Kicker.

'About half an hour each,' he said. 'But we've got plenty of spare fuel. When the back row runs out I'll replace them with fresh ones. And if they all run out I'll kick 'em the rest of the way!'

The beach receded in the distance, as did the Brown Forest. Zack was very happy to see the back of it, although now the sea posed a new challenge. He'd only been on the raft for a few minutes and he was already feeling seasick. He put his hand up to his mouth.

Zack lay down next to Eleanor, who was sitting at the front of the raft, staring into the water.

Eleanor looked at Zack.

'Are you all right?' she said. 'Your face has gone green.'

Zack shrugged. 'Could be better,' he said. 'How about you?'

'I'm okay,' she said. 'Just wish I could locate my father. I reckon we're going to need him.'

'So you've got no idea where he is?' said Zack.

'No,' said Eleanor. 'And it's just not like him to leave without telling me where he was going.'

'What about your mum?' said Zack. 'Did he say anything to her?'

Eleanor shook her head.

'I don't have a mum,' she said. 'Not any more. She was killed when I was five years old.'

Zack was shocked. He didn't know what to say.

'That's terrible,' he finally mumbled. 'How?'

Eleanor took a deep breath.

'We were having a picnic,' she said. 'I remember Dad was being silly. He was juggling boiled eggs and Mum and I were laughing at him. Next thing I knew Mum was lying on her back. Not moving. Not breathing. I looked up. We were surrounded by bums. And in the middle stood the most evil bum of them all.'

'Stenchgantor?' said Zack.

'No,' said Eleanor. 'He's the smelliest, but he's not the most evil. Not evil in the way the Great White Bum is evil.'

'The Great White Bum!' said Zack.

'It was payback for my father's role in putting an end to a bum uprising the month before,' said Eleanor. 'Lots of bums were killed. The whole B-team was involved, but the Great White Bum held my father directly responsible.'

'Did it try to kill you as well?' said Zack.

'Oh, yes,' said Eleanor. 'But Dad saved me. He fought the bums, including the Great White Bum, single-handedly. But he couldn't save Mum. It was too late.'

Zack shook his head, trying to imagine what it must feel like to have your mum murdered by the Great White Bum. Then he had an idea.

'Do you think the Great White Bum has anything to do with the bumcano?' he said.

'I don't only *think* so,' said Eleanor. 'I *know* so. Wherever there's trouble the Great White Bum is never far away. I wouldn't be surprised if it's masterminding the whole uprising.'

Zack wasn't sure whether to feel relieved that his bum might not be completely responsible for the mad plan to take over the world, or whether to be even more worried. The thought that his bum might be in league with the Great White Bum was pretty frightening.

He looked down into the water. It was teaming with exotic bum-fish, the likes of which he'd never even dreamed existed. Bums with teeth, with fins, with tails and scales. A bum with three eyes. A spotted bum-shark. An octobum with cheeks elongated into vast thin wings glided under the raft and then disappeared into the depths. It was all so strange. There was so much he didn't know. Zack felt completely out of his depth.

The Smacker tapped Zack on the shoulder.

'Here,' she said.

He turned around.

She was holding four of the bum-plugging corks, and four smaller corks.

'Take two of the big ones,' she said, and stick them in your ears. 'Put the little ones up your nose. And don't remove them until I tell you to. Got that?'

She gave the other set to Eleanor.

'But why?' said Zack.

'There are many beautiful things in the Sea of Bums,' said the Smacker. 'But they can also be deadly. And the most beautiful and deadliest of all are the Siren Bums.'

'Siren Bums?' said Zack.

'Bums that live on small rocky outcrops in the Sea of Bums,' said the Smacker. 'They have such a sweet scent and such a beautiful song that all who hear and smell them forget all thoughts of their mission, their families, friends and home, and are compelled to jump overboard. They have only one thought in their minds—to spend the rest of their lives drinking in the song and the smell and the beauty of the Siren Bums. Sadly, they never make it that far. They are torn to pieces and eaten by the abundant sea-bum life that you see all around us.'

As if to emphasise what the Smacker had just said, Zack noticed a large red-spotted bum-shark rise up through the depths, roll to one side, reveal a frightening set of teeth and head back down into the dark water.

Zack took the plugs.

'Thanks,' he said.

He turned to Eleanor.

'Have you ever heard the Siren Bums sing?' he said.

She didn't reply.

'Eleanor?' said Zack.

Her head was turned away. He wondered if he'd upset her in some way. He tapped her shoulder. She turned around and Zack repeated his question.

'I'm sorry, Zack,' she said in a loud voice. 'I can't hear a thing you're saying. I've got the plugs in my ears!'

'Okay, okay,' said Zack. 'You don't have to shout!'

'Pardon?' said Eleanor.

Zack shrugged. 'Don't worry about it,' he said.

'What?' said Eleanor.

'I've heard them,' said the Kicker, who obviously didn't have his earplugs in.

'You've heard the Siren Bums?' said Zack.

'Yeah,' said the Kicker. 'Beautiful too. Most amazing thing I ever heard.'

'But how did you survive?' said Zack.

The Kicker laughed and winked.

'Takes more than a singing bum to get the better of me,' he said. 'They're not *that* dangerous. But they are worth hearing. At least once.'

It was one of the few times since Zack had met him that the Kicker had talked about something other than kicking bums. He figured the sound of the Siren Bums must be pretty special. Zack had only ever known bums to make crude, disgusting noises. The noises were occasionally amusing, of course, but Zack couldn't remember a single one that he would have called beautiful. Was it possible they really did sound like the Kicker described?

Zack rolled the plugs in between his fingers, trying to decide whether to take the Smacker at her word or to take a chance and believe the Kicker.

That's when he heard it.

Just a faint sound at first, almost indistinguishable from the roar of the bum-raft, but definitely there. And definitely beautiful. Like a beautiful choir. Like a choir of angels, thought Zack.

He could see a small rocky outcrop ahead. There were three bums on it, smooth and round and pink like ripe peaches.

And the smell was something else again. It was like Zack's nostrils had died and gone to heaven. Sweet and fruity, it wafted all around him. He sniffed deeply, and then sniffed again, trying to take in as much of the smell as he could, but it wasn't enough. He wanted to get closer. He *had* to get closer.

Zack couldn't stay on the raft any more. All he cared about was the sound and the smell of the Siren Bums. He had to get to them.

Nothing else was important.

Not food.

Not water.

Not family.

Not the B-team.

Not Eleanor.

And definitely not his bum.
Only the Siren Bums.
They were all that mattered.
Zack jumped into the water and started swimming.

CHAPTER SEVEN

POOPOISES AND GIANT BLOWFLIES

O r so Zack was told later, anyway.
He didn't remember jumping. All he remembered
was waking up with the Smacker sitting on his chest,
Eleanor sitting on his legs and the Kisser pinching his
nose, pulling his head back and about to put his mouth
over Zack's.

'What are you doing?!' spluttered Zack, spitting
out seawater.

The Kisser pulled back.

'Trying to save your life,' he said.

'Huh?' said Zack

'You kept jumping in, you idiot!' said Eleanor.

Zack shook his head. 'I did?'

'Only five times,' she said. 'You nearly drowned.'

'I'm sorry,' stammered Zack, beginning to feel very
stupid. 'Sorry if I've been any trouble.'

'Trouble?' said the Smacker. 'Trouble? No trouble
at all! Feel free to disregard my instructions and risk

your life and everybody else's life anytime you feel like it! Why didn't you put your earplugs in like I told you?'

'I was going to,' said Zack, 'but the Kicker told me that the Siren Bums were worth hearing at least once.'

The Kicker glared at Zack.

The Smacker turned on the Kicker.

'Is that true?' she said.

'Look at that sky!' said the Kicker. 'There's going to be a storm.'

'Answer the question!' said the Smacker. 'Is it true?'

The Kicker shuffled uncomfortably under the Smacker's glare. 'Yes,' he said. 'It was a test.'

'A test?' said the Smacker. 'What sort of test?'

'An intelligence test,' said the Kicker. 'Which he failed.'

'He could have been killed!' said the Smacker.

The Kicker was looking up at the sky again. 'That's one almighty storm blowing our way,' he said.

Zack looked up.

Sure enough the sky was an enormous black swirling cauldron of storm clouds. Big clouds. Brutal clouds. The kind of clouds you wouldn't like to meet on a street late at night.

'Do you think we'll get there before the storm hits?' said the Smacker.

'Hard to say,' said the Kicker. 'I reckon we're only about halfway. And that storm looks mean.'

As he spoke the wind gusted violently against their faces, whipping up the swell to almost twice its previous height. Zack watched as the clouds crashed and merged, forming even bigger and more brutal clouds.

'Can't we go any faster?' said the Kisser.

'We could try uncorking the second row as well,' said the Kicker. 'More than that I wouldn't like to risk. The raft could break apart.'

'It's worth a try,' said the Smacker. 'Eleanor, keep your eye on Zack. Make sure he doesn't try to jump in again.'

The Smacker and the Kisser set to uncorking the bums in the second row.

While they did that, Eleanor drew Zack aside.

'Is it true what you said about the Kicker?' she said.

'Yes,' said Zack.

Eleanor shook her head.

'I don't know why he would say that,' she said. 'He knows how dangerous those Siren Bums are . . . unless . . .'

She hesitated.

'Unless what?' said Zack.

Eleanor looked at Zack, and then spoke in a very low voice. 'Unless he really *did* want to kill you.'

The bum-raft rose into the air on a particularly large swell and dropped again. Just like Zack's stomach.

'But why would he want to kill me?' said Zack, beginning to feel sick again.

Eleanor looked around her to make sure nobody was listening and then leaned in close to Zack.

'I've had my doubts about him for a while now,' she said. 'I think he's up to something.'

'What?' said Zack.

'I'm not sure,' said Eleanor. 'He's just been acting strangely, that's all. Like when he sent me to find you in the Brown Forest. He didn't even offer to come with me.'

'Maybe he just doesn't like me,' said Zack.

'I think it's more than that,' said Eleanor. 'I think he's trying to sabotage our mission. I don't think he was expecting either of us to make it out of the Brown Forest alive.'

Zack looked at the sky. The clouds seemed to have all joined into one gigantic cloud. Big. Black. Evil. The wind was getting stronger by the minute and the sea around the raft was bubbling and churning like a giant washing machine.

'He did seem pretty surprised to see us,' said Zack, swallowing as hard as he could.

'Exactly,' said Eleanor. She paused. 'I think he might be a bum sympathiser.'

'No way,' said Zack, clutching the side of the raft as it dropped to the bottom of a large wave and rose again almost as quickly. 'He hates bums.'

'So he says,' says Eleanor. 'A little too often, don't you think? Maybe he just says that to try to cover up the truth. And maybe he's trying to kill you because he's scared that you'll be able to talk your bum out of going through with its plan.'

Zack struggled to take in what Eleanor was telling him. The Kicker, one of the world's greatest bum-fighters, a bum sympathiser? It was impossible. And yet Zack couldn't deny that what Eleanor said seemed to square with the facts.

'So what do you think we should do?' said Zack.

'Right now there's nothing we can do,' said Eleanor. 'It's going to be difficult to convince the others until we have some hard evidence. In the meantime, just be careful. He might try again.'

Eleanor looked around to make sure none of the others were watching. Then she reached down, rolled up her trouser leg and removed a small bum-gun strapped above her left ankle. She passed it to Zack.

'Here, take this,' she said. 'You probably need it more than I do.'

Zack put the gun in the front pouch of his belt. 'Thanks,' he said. He hoped he wouldn't have to use it, but it made him feel better knowing it was there.

The wind roared and howled. The storm was setting in fast. Zack looked up and saw a large wave.

A *very* large wave.

The wall of water seemed to rise forever . . . and then it started to break. An avalanche of white foam came tumbling down the face of the wave towards the tiny raft.

'Hold tight, everybody,' yelled the Smacker.

Zack flattened himself against the bum-raft, wedged his hands in between two of the biggest pairs of cheeks he could find and braced himself.

The wave slammed down on top of them.

Zack had never felt anything like it.

He was washed clear of the raft and sent somersaulting helplessly into the depths of the bum ocean.

Zack was under the water for a long time before he surfaced.

When he finally did surface there was no sign of the bum-raft.

Just the Kicker, the Smacker, the Kisser and Eleanor all fighting for their lives in the foaming craziness around them.

'I thought you said the raft was unsinkable!' said the Kisser as the Kicker floated in front of him.

'It was,' said the Kicker.

'Then how come it sunk?' said the Kisser.

'It didn't sink,' said the Kicker. 'It broke apart. How was I to know that there'd be freak waves like that?'

Zack glanced at Eleanor. She glanced back.

She was right, thought Zack. The Kicker really *was* trying to sabotage the mission.

Zack gulped.

They were in the middle of the Sea of Bums. They had no raft. They were going to drown. And if they didn't drown, they'd be killed by the Kicker who was clearly hellbent on eliminating them all.

Zack calmly assessed the situation and then did the only thing possible.

He panicked.

'We're doomed!' he yelled. 'We're going to die! We're all going to die!'

The Smacker swam over, grabbed Zack and slapped his face.

'Get a grip, boy!' she yelled. 'You're not dead yet are you?'

Zack shook his head.

'No,' he said, 'but . . .'

'But nothing!' yelled the Smacker above the howling

wind. 'We've still got a world to save! You can die later, if you want, but not now. And that's an order!'

Zack nodded meekly.

He didn't want her to slap him again.

Besides, he thought. She was right. They *weren't* dead yet. And the storm seemed to be easing slightly. There was still hope.

That's when Zack saw them.

Fins.

Triangular shaped dorsal fins cutting through the water towards them.

Zack started to panic again.

The Smacker was wrong.

They *were* going to die.

'Help!' screamed Zack. 'Sharks!'

The others spun around and saw the rapidly approaching fleet of fins.

'Don't worry!' said the Smacker. 'I'll smack them if they come near us.'

'And I'll kick their bums,' said the Kicker.

Everyone looked to the Kisser, who stared back blankly. 'Well, don't look at me,' he said. 'I'm not kissing them. Not with those teeth!'

As they watched and held their breath, one of the creatures leapt out of the sea. It rose gracefully into the air and then dived back into the water. Zack blinked. He didn't know much about the creatures that lived in the Sea of Bums, but he knew enough to realise that this was obviously not a shark. It looked more like a porpoise except that its skin was a dimpled glossy brown rather than the usual porpoise-grey.

'Nobody smack or kick or do anything to them,' cried Eleanor.

'Why not?' said the Smacker.

'Because they're not sharks.'

'Then what are they?' said Zack.

Eleanor smiled broadly and stretched out her hand to pat one that was headed straight for her. 'They're poopoises,' she said.

'You mean porpoises?' said Zack.

'No,' she said, patting the large brown creature as it playfully ducked and dived around her. '*Poo*poises! And they're friendly. Just put your arms around its neck and it will carry you to shore.'

'There's no way I'm putting my arms around a poopoise!' said Zack.

But nobody heard him.

They had already each grabbed a poopoise and were rocketing off into the distance.

One of the remaining poopoises nudged Zack's arm.

He pulled away. But then Zack started to feel the water sucking him under again and he looked up to see another huge wave—even bigger than the wave that had destroyed the bum-raft. And it was about to break right on top of him.

Zack had no choice. He grabbed the poopoise and barely had time to catch his breath before it shot off down into the water, away from the killer wave.

The poopoise re-emerged in the wake of the others, diving effortlessly through the raging sea.

After a while Zack worked up the confidence to get up and sit on the poopoise's back, using its dorsal fin as a handhold. This allowed the poopoise to move even faster, and pretty soon he'd caught up to the others.

'Wow, look at you go!' said Eleanor, as Zack pulled up alongside her. 'Anyone would think you've been riding poopoises all your life.'

'Nothing to it, really,' said Zack. 'Watch this!'

He lay flat on the poopoise and then pushed himself up, brought up his legs and stood up. He was surfing!

Without Zack's legs dragging in the water, the poopoise was able to swim even faster and pretty soon Zack was way ahead of the group.

Then, through the angry spray of the storm, Zack saw it.

The bumcano.

It rose dark and black against the twilight—its smoothly sloping sides rising till they were almost parallel at the top. Well, mostly smooth, except for a lumpy outcrop about three-quarters of the way up on the left-hand side.

The bumcano seemed to take up most of the island.

A dark, sinister presence in the middle of a dark, sinister sea.

Zack lowered himself back down to a sitting position.

He didn't want to be the first one there.

No way.

As Zack drew closer, two things became noticeable.

Firstly, the smell.

It was like all the sewage farms in the world put together. Only worse. Ten million times worse, to be exact. If Zack's nose could have run away it would have done so right at that moment.

The second thing Zack noticed was the ring of black shapes circling the top of the bumcano.

'What are those things flying around the top?' Zack said to Eleanor.

'I'm not sure,' she said. 'But I don't like the look of them.'

As the group neared the beach, the black shapes stopped circling the bumcano and started flying down towards them.

The eye of the storm was now far behind them, and the howling winds were replaced by a loud buzzing noise.

'Oh no,' said Eleanor. 'My dad used to tell me stories about these, but I always thought he was making them up to scare me.'

'They sound like blowflies,' said Zack.

'That's because they *are* blowflies,' said Eleanor. '*Giant* blowflies! And here they come!'

'All right, listen up,' yelled the Smacker. 'Form an attack circle. Kicker—you go on my right. Kisser—you take the left. Eleanor—go directly behind me.'

'What about me?' yelled Zack as the others took their positions.

'Keep as low as you can,' said the Smacker. 'Leave this to us.'

Before Zack could argue he saw one of the giant

blowflies heading straight for him—its huge coppery eyes as big as dinner plates and a proboscis as long and thick as an elephant's trunk.

That was the last thing Zack saw before the fly vomited. A thick stream of sticky yellowish-green goo splattered all over Zack and his poopoise.

Zack's poopoise dived down deep under the water. The water helped to wash most of the disgusting gunk off both of them. They re-emerged about fifty metres away from the B-team's attack circle, the air above the fighting force now thick with giant blowflies. Not that the B-team seemed particularly worried. Zack marvelled at the ruthless efficiency with which they were dispatching the blowflies.

The Kicker was crouching on the back of his poopoise, his arms folded across his chest. He was kicking with one foot and then the other, and sometimes leaping up into the air and kicking with both feet at once. He looked more like a Russian Cossack dancer than a bum-fighter.

The Smacker's arms were a blur, cutting, dicing and chopping the flies like helicopter blades. She looked like a human blender making a giant blowfly smoothie.

The Kisser was expending the least effort of any of them, but was no less deadly for that. He sat on his poopoise simply plucking the blowflies from the air, kissing them between the eyes and then dropping them into the water.

Eleanor seemed to be using a combination of both hands and feet—kick-boxer style. She wasn't killing as many blowflies as any of the B-team but her broad smile suggested that she was enjoying herself.

The sea around them was thick with green and yellow goo.

But just when it looked like the B-team had the situation under control, a new wave of giant blowflies began to pour out of the bumcano—and these blowflies were even bigger, louder and more plentiful than the first wave.

Their situation looked hopeless.

No matter how talented or determined the B-team were, Zack could see they were outnumbered. It was only a matter of time before they would all become maggot-food.

The Smacker recognised it too.

'Head for the shore!' she yelled. 'There are too many of them. It's our only chance! Zack, follow us!'

The B-team raced towards the island. Zack did the same. He stood up on his poopoise and surfed after them.

He saw Eleanor turn around.

'Get down!' she yelled, pointing into the sky above him.

Zack looked up, saw the dark wet end of a blowfly proboscis, and then everything went black.

He felt himself being lifted up into the air by his head.

Zack had been through some pretty disgusting experiences in the past few days, but this had to be the most disgusting experience of all. It was also the most painful because at the same time as he was being sucked upwards into the fly's proboscis someone was pulling him downwards by his legs. He was being pulled from both ends and felt like he was going to snap in the middle. This must be how a rubber band feels, thought Zack, just before it breaks.

Just when he thought he couldn't take it any more Zack felt the force pulling on his legs win out and his head was pulled free of the slimy proboscis and he splashed down into the sea.

As Zack came up for air he saw the Kisser reach up and pluck the fly out of the sky. It immediately stopped its angry buzzing and started crooning like a dove—its whole body softening and relaxing as the Kisser stroked the wiry tufts of hair that sprouted out from between its eyes. Then the Kisser puckered up, kissed the fly in the middle of its forehead and gently pushed it down into the water and held it under until it stopped kicking.

Zack was impressed by the Kisser's style.

'Thanks!' said Zack. 'I owe you one!'

'Just doing my job,' said the Kisser wiping his mouth with his handkerchief. 'Come on. We'd better get moving.'

Zack remounted his poopoise and he and the Kisser followed the rest of the B-team towards the shore, which was barely visible through the black haze of flies.

As they reached the beach the poopoises all stopped and bucked their riders off.

Zack didn't want to leave his poopoise—not only was it his only protection against the blowflies, but he'd grown fond of it. His poopoise, however, obviously didn't feel the same way. It bucked him off into the shallows, turned around and swam away.

Zack put his arms over his head and started running

as fast as he could, expecting to be covered in yellow-green goo and sucked up into another giant blowfly's proboscis at any moment.

But it didn't happen.

'Look!' said Eleanor, who was beside him.

Zack stopped and looked around.

There were no blowflies.

They were all in a thick clump far out to sea, chasing the poopoises. 'It must have been them they wanted all along,' said Zack.

Eleanor's eyes were full of tears.

'Those poopoises risked their lives for us,' she said.

Zack, Eleanor and the B-team stood on the beach and watched the poopoises until they disappeared, taking the entire pack of giant blowflies with them.

'The flies must have been breeding inside the bumcano,' said the Smacker. 'Not surprising, really. The conditions would make an ideal nursery.'

Zack shuddered at the thought of the size of the maggots that would be produced by the gigantic flies that had been attacking them. The thought of a bumcano full of them made him break out in a cold sweat.

He looked around. They were standing on a narrow strip of beach bordered by thick jungle. The jungle consisted mostly of bumnut trees, which closely resembled coconut trees, except for the bumnuts, which, as their name suggested, looked more like bums than coconuts. The jungle was alive with hoots and chattering sounds. As strange as it was, Zack preferred it to the eerie silence of the Brown Forest.

'What's making that racket?' he said.

'Feral bums,' said Eleanor. 'Bum-jungles like this are full of them.'

But the most amazing thing about the island was the bumcano. It was an awesome sight. It rose up out of the jungle and towered over everything. On top Zack could see that there was a main crater, and a little way down on one side was another, smaller opening. There were shimmering stink-waves coming out of both holes.

'We've got to get that bumcano plugged as soon as we can,' said the Smacker. 'Judging by the warmth of the ground and the size of those flies it must be pretty full already.'

Zack knelt down and felt the ground.

The Smacker was right.

It was very warm.

Zack knew from studying volcanoes at school that somewhere deep below a volcano there is usually a huge chamber where the molten rock collects. Only in this case it wasn't molten rock. It was much worse. And it was breaking down. Composting. Heating up the whole island.

'How are we going to plug it?' said Zack. 'It's huge.'

The Smacker nodded.

'It's not going to be easy, but a couple of nuclear bums should do the trick. One for the top of the bumcano and one for the side vent. We just need to collect enough feral bums, bind them together and then build a catapult to fire them up there. They'll explode and create enough debris to seal up the bumcano forever.'

'But the bums will still be inside,' said Eleanor. 'They'll just keep going until they've got even more power—enough to blow the plugs out and create even more devastation.'

'If you've got a better idea, then let's hear it,' said the Smacker.

'I say we go in there and find my dad,' said Eleanor.

'Are you joking?' said the Smacker. 'There are too many bums in there! We'll be outnumbered twenty to one!'

'But my father could be in there as well,' said Eleanor.

'You don't know that for sure,' said the Kicker.

'You don't know for sure that he isn't,' said Eleanor.

'No,' said the Smacker, 'but if he was I know he wouldn't want us going in there on some damn fool rescue mission. He'd want us to do it my way.'

'No,' said Eleanor, her eyes flashing with anger, 'he'd want us to do it properly, not put bandaids over the top and hope they go away. He'd want us to deal with the problem at its source.'

'You mean try to talk to my bum?' said Zack.

'I'm sorry, Zack,' said Eleanor. 'But your bum is insane. It has to be terminated. It's the only safe way.'

'But what if it's not just my bum?' said Zack. 'What if the Great White Bum is involved as well?'

'Then we kill that too,' said Eleanor.

She turned to the group.

'Don't you see?' she pleaded. 'We've got it cornered. We'll never get a better chance to make sure it never pulls this or any other stunt ever again.'

'So that's what this is about,' said the Smacker.

'What do you mean?' said Eleanor.

'Getting even with the Great White Bum.'

'No,' said Eleanor. 'That's got nothing to do with it.'

'It's got everything to do with it!' said the Smacker angrily. 'Listen to yourself. Listen to what you're proposing. I know what that bum did to you and your father, Eleanor. I know what it took away from you both. But you're letting emotion cloud your better judgment. I want to rid the world of the Great White Bum as much as you do, but dying won't help us achieve that.'

'Who said anything about dying?' said Eleanor. 'We got this far. If we work as a team we can make it the rest of the way. Why chicken out now?'

'We only got this far by the grace of God and a fair measure of good luck,' said the Smacker. 'But it can't hold out forever. The bumcano is too steep. Too high. Too dangerous. And that's not even taking into account the danger of going inside a bumcano full of bums. We plug it, and that's final.'

There was silence.

Zack watched as the Kicker stepped forward.

'I agree with the Smacker,' he said. 'I want to kick bum as much as you do, Eleanor, but there's no point in killing ourselves.'

'No,' said the Kisser. 'There is no point in killing ourselves, but I don't think that's what Eleanor is proposing. We've spent the last twenty years risking our lives fighting bum uprisings all over the planet and we all know who has been behind every single one of them. Eleanor's right. We don't know for sure that the Great White Bum is behind this, but it's highly likely that it is. We've got the Great White Bum cornered. We'll never get a better chance to finish it off once and for all. We're a highly trained bum-fighting outfit. If we can't figure out a way to pool our resources and get ourselves up that bumcano then we're not worthy of the name "B-team". I say we go in.'

Everyone was silent. They all looked at Eleanor.

Finally she spoke.

'Well, Zack,' she said. 'Looks like it's a tie. Two all. I guess that gives you the deciding vote.'

Zack gulped. He looked at the Smacker. She nodded.

'All right,' she said. 'Let Zack decide. After all, it is his bum in there.'

Zack didn't know what to do.

He didn't want to die any more than anybody else, but he knew that going in would at least give him a chance to talk to his bum and convince it to surrender peacefully.

But maybe it was too late for that. Perhaps Eleanor was right. It was time to face facts. His bum was psycho. It would probably always be psycho. His false bum had given him no trouble at all. And it *was* self-wiping. He could go back home and live a safe, predictable life, free from the tyranny of his wayward bum. Plugging his bum inside the bumcano would be cruel and horrible, he knew that, but so was what it was threatening to do to the world. And it only had itself to blame. Zack had done everything he could. Besides which, he trusted the Smacker's judgment.

'Well?' said Eleanor.

'Plug it,' he whispered.

Eleanor's face turned bright red.

She shook her head in disbelief and stormed off down the beach.

Zack shrugged at the group and ran after her.

'Eleanor,' he said. 'Wait! Let me explain!'

'You don't have to explain anything,' she said. 'You're an idiot—that explains everything!'

'At least I'm not a know-it-all!' said Zack, who'd had enough of Eleanor's superior attitude.

Eleanor wheeled around.

'I'd rather be a know-it-all than an *idiot*!' she yelled. 'Did you happen to notice who else you just voted with? The Kicker. The man who tried to kill you. The double-agent.'

'We don't know that for sure,' said Zack. 'You said yourself we have no hard evidence.'

Eleanor snorted.

'You are so thick!' she said. 'How much more evidence do you need? The fact that he voted not to go into the bumcano *proves* that he's a double-agent. He knows I'm right. He knows that plugging the bumcano would solve nothing. He's on the bums' side—not ours.'

Zack had an awful sinking feeling.

Like he'd just stuffed up again. Big time.

He wanted to go back and have his vote again. But it was too late.

'I'm sorry,' he said.

'So am I,' said Eleanor, and she turned and walked away.

Zack felt bad about his decision but he didn't have much time to worry about it. The rest of what was left of the afternoon was taken up with pulling bumnut tree saplings out of the ground, collecting jungle twine and trapping bums.

By nightfall they had made a bum-cage and filled it with forty feral bums—enough to make at least two nuclear bums. Zack watched as the bums bounced off the walls, the floor and the ceiling of their cage, hooting and calling the whole time. The smell was appalling, almost as bad as the smell emanating from the bumcano.

Near the cage were two nuclear bum launchers. They were made out of two long, springy bumnut saplings at the edge of the jungle, the tops of which had been bent right over until they were almost touching the ground. All that was stopping them from springing back up was a short length of jungle twine. One tree was aimed in the direction of the main bumcano shaft. The other at the vent on its side. When the nuclear bums were cradled in the top of the tree and the twine was cut, the trees would spring back up and, like cata-pults, hurl the nuclear bums at their respective targets. Zack had to hand it to the B-team: they really seemed to know what they were doing.

As it grew dark they sat around a campfire eating

roasted bumnuts. The nutty wood tasted slightly like burnt toast, but it was the first real food they'd had since their rations had disappeared in the tornado so nobody was complaining.

Behind them the jungle was alive with the calls of feral bums. Luckily the smoke from their campfire masked their stink as well as the terrible stench of the bumcano.

'We'll launch the nuclear bums at first light tomorrow morning,' said the Smacker, throwing a handful of bumnut husks into the fire and causing sparks to leap high into the black tropical night sky.

'I say we do it tonight,' said the Kicker, spitting bumnut shells onto the ground in front of him. 'Why waste time?'

'There's not enough light now,' said the Smacker. 'We wouldn't be able to aim the catapults accurately.'

Zack looked across the fire at Eleanor. She was sitting there sullenly, not saying a word. She had built the fire, but had made a point of not helping with any of the nuclear bum preparations. She was still furious with Zack and wouldn't catch his eye.

Zack lay down, stretched out his legs and looked up at the stars. He tried to pick out the familiar constellations that his grandmother had showed him: the saucepan, the Southern Cross and the Scorpion . . . but he recognised nothing. The only shapes he could make out were bums. Big bums. Small bums. Orion's bum. A sky full of bums.

Zack wondered if he would ever see his bum again. It was probably too late now, but despite everything it had put him through, he still missed it.

The previous forty-eight hours had taken their toll though and before Zack could miss his bum too much, he closed his eyes and fell asleep.

When Zack woke it was light.

The Kisser was shaking him roughly by the shoulder. 'Wake up, Zack!' he said. 'Have you seen Eleanor?'

'Huh?' said Zack.

He opened his eyes and looked around.

He saw that the campfire was out. And the stink of the bumcano was back in full force. Then he noticed the feral bum-cage. It was empty.

The Smacker sat up, rubbing her eyes. 'Oh no,' she said. 'And the feral bums have gone too.'

They looked at the cage. The door was wide open.

The Smacker punched the Kicker, who was still lying beside the fire, snoring loudly.

'Wake up!' she said. 'We've got a situation.'

'Eleanor must have let them out,' said the Kisser.

'But why would she do that?' said the Smacker. 'It doesn't make sense. She hates bums.'

'Maybe they tricked her,' said the Kisser.

'She was on their side all along!' said the Kicker who was pulling his boots on. 'I knew it! She's a bum sympathiser. I'm going to kick her bum!'

'If you can catch her,' said the Kisser. 'Look—the bum launcher pointing towards the main shaft has been fired. Maybe they used it to send her up into the bumcano as a human sacrifice. We have to rescue her!'

'But Eleanor is a smart kid,' said the Smacker. 'It just doesn't make sense that the bums could trick her. She's the Bum Hunter's daughter after all!'

'She's been under a lot of pressure,' said the Kisser. 'We all have. It's easy to make a small error of judgment.'

'This is not a small error—this is a *major* error!' said the Smacker. 'It's just not like her. It could be a trap. We go running in there to save her and they cream us.'

'I think you're both wrong,' said Zack. 'She was pretty cut up about the decision not to go into the bumcano. I reckon she's catapulted herself inside and gone to find her father.'

'Now *that* sounds more like Eleanor,' said the Smacker, slamming a fist into her hand out of frustration. 'She probably let the feral bums out to give herself more time. She knows it's going to take us at least a couple of hours to collect new ones.'

'But surely we're not going to go ahead with that plan now,' said the Kisser. 'We have to go and help her.'

'I say we collect new bums and proceed as planned,' said the Kicker angrily.

'But you'll kill Eleanor,' said Zack.

'Better she dies than everybody in the whole world gets rearranged!' said the Kicker. 'She's not stupid. She must have known the risk she was taking.'

'Maybe,' said the Kisser quietly. 'But Zack's right. We have to go in there.'

The Smacker nodded.

'All right!' said the Kicker. 'But don't say I didn't warn you.'

Eleanor was right about the Kicker, thought Zack. He must be a double-agent. Not only had he tried to kill Zack in the Sea of Bums, but here he was openly suggesting that they condemn Eleanor to certain death. Zack recalled Eleanor's warning. He was going to have to watch the Kicker very carefully.

'We're going to need plenty of twine,' said the Smacker. 'We'll have to climb.'

'Why don't we use the other nuclear bum launcher?' said Zack.

'Too much guess-work,' said the Smacker. Near enough is good enough for a nuclear bum—but not for us. You could fall short, long—or, worst of all, get a hole in one and go straight down the bumcano's main shaft—nothing to slow you down—straight into the . . .'

'How do we know Eleanor made it?' Zack said quickly before the Smacker could finish. He didn't want to have to imagine such a gruesome fate for any-one—especially not Eleanor.

'We don't,' said the Smacker, shrugging. 'She could be lying injured on the far side of the bum-cano for all we know. But we won't be much help to her if we end up lying next to her with the same injuries.'

Zack and the B-team were soon hacking their way through the jungle. Zack looked around him. He knew something was different, but couldn't figure out what. Then he realised. There were no bum noises. In fact, there were no bums. Not anywhere.

'What happened to all the ferals?' he said.

'Probably massing in the bumcano with the other bums,' said the Kisser. 'Their hour of triumph must be near—they probably all want to be a part of it.'

There was something about the way the Kisser said 'hour of triumph' that sent shivers down Zack's spine. The thought that bums might soon be ruling the world was truly horrifying. Up till now Zack had clung to the hope that he still might be able to talk some sense into his bum. Now he wasn't so sure. There wasn't much time left and if Eleanor was right, maybe it wasn't just his bum running the show anyway.

After fifteen minutes of hacking and slashing they arrived at the bottom of the bumcano. In front of them was an almost vertical slab of black rock.

'We'll head up towards the side vent,' said the Smacker. 'It will take a little longer, but it's not as steep. From there it will be a short climb to the top and then we can abseil down into the main vent.'

The Kicker and the Kisser both nodded.

'But how do we get up?' said Zack. 'It's too steep. And there are no handholds.'

The Smacker smiled.

'I'll soon fix that,' she said, tying a length of twine around her waist.

She stepped up to the rock-face, jumped up and smacked it hard. A number of small hairline fractures appeared in the rock. The Smacker jumped and smacked it a few more times until the impact had caused one of the fractures to grow into a crack big enough for her to wedge the fingers of her right hand into. She pulled herself up and, still hanging, started smacking the rock above her with her left hand. It was slow-going, but it was the only way they had.

The Kicker followed, making the cracks even bigger by applying an explosive kick to each of them.

Zack was next and the Kisser brought up the rear.

Crack by crack, Zack fought his way up the bumcano. But even with the help of the handholds and the Smacker's rope it was hard work.

They climbed solidly for two hours without talking. Some sections of the climb were easier than others, but by the time the side vent came into view Zack's fingers were raw and bleeding. However, he still had to climb a final vertical slab of rock, more sheer and difficult than anything he had encountered so far. The Smacker climbed this section by herself and then threw down a length of jungle twine for the Kicker to pull himself up with.

Then it was Zack's turn. By the time he made it to the top of the rock-face he was exhausted.

The Smacker reached down and pulled him up over the ledge. Zack collapsed onto his back and lay there staring up at the dark steaming mouth of the side vent, his chest heaving. He noted with relief that from here the top of the bumcano was not far and that there was no more vertical climbing—just a steeply graded slope. He could also see the Kicker was a few hundred metres up the slope. Zack was studying the Kicker closely for any signs of suspicious behaviour when he heard screaming coming from below the shelf. He stood up and looked over the edge.

He was shocked to see the Kisser hanging onto the edge of the rock-face by one hand, his legs dangling and kicking over the long drop below.

'Don't panic,' said the Smacker who was trying to grab the Kisser's free arm. 'Try to concentrate and give me your hand!'

She knelt down and extended her powerful arm towards him.

Zack couldn't see exactly what happened next because the Smacker was in front of him, blocking his view of the Kisser.

All he knew was that suddenly the Smacker screamed, tumbled forward and disappeared over the edge.

Zack heard her scream. He heard her scream until she fell out of range and he couldn't hear her any more.

CHAPTER EIGHT

THE BUMCANO

Zack was stunned.

The Smacker? Dead? It was impossible!

He looked around for the Kicker, who was running back down the slope towards him.

The Kisser managed to pull himself over the ledge just as the Kicker arrived. He lay on the ground, breathing hard.

'What happened to the Smacker?' said the Kicker.

'She seemed to lose her balance,' said the Kisser, panting. 'She was helping me up . . . and she slipped. I tried to save her . . . but I couldn't do anything. She fell.'

The Kicker was staring down at the Kisser. 'Get up,' he said coldly.

'I beg your pardon?' said the Kisser.

'Get up so I can kick your bum,' said the Kicker. 'Like I should have done a long time ago.'

'Look,' said the Kisser, standing up, 'I know you're

upset. I am too, but at a time like this we have to stick together. We're mates, remember?'

'You're no mate of mine,' said the Kicker. 'You killed the Smacker!'

'Don't be ridiculous,' said the Kisser. 'It was an accident. Wasn't it, Zack? You saw it.'

But Zack couldn't speak. He was still too shocked. Besides, he hadn't seen exactly what happened. All he knew was that one moment the Smacker was there and the next moment she wasn't.

'Accident, my bum,' said the Kicker. 'The Smacker was a great bum warrior. She doesn't just fall off the edge of a cliff for no reason. Not unless she was *pulled* over.'

'Think about what you're saying!' said the Kisser.

'I have thought about it,' said the Kicker. 'I've had my suspicions about you for a long time. And now I'm going to kick your bum.'

'What are you trying to say?' said the Kisser. 'That I'm on their side?'

The Kicker's only reply was to come sailing through the air and kick the Kisser in the stomach. The Kisser staggered backwards, almost over the cliff.

'No, Kicker!' yelled Zack, finding his voice. He knew one of them was a double-agent, he just wasn't sure *which* one. He'd thought it was the Kicker, but after what had just happened to the Smacker, he wasn't so sure any more. Then again, perhaps it really *had* been an accident.

'Keep out of it,' said the Kicker over his shoulder. 'This is between me and him.'

The Kisser leapt to his feet. 'Please, Kicker,' he said, stepping away from the cliff edge, 'you're making a big mistake.'

But the Kicker ignored him and moved in closer, circling like a shark.

The Kisser raised his hand to his mouth, kissed it, and then blew the kiss at the Kicker.

The Kicker ducked, as if dodging a bullet.

'Cut it out!' he yelled. 'Fight like a man, you lousy bum sympathiser!'

The Kicker charged forward and kicked, but was blocked in midair by another one of the Kisser's hand-kisses. He fell to the ground with a crash.

Zack knew he had to do something. He had to stop them before they destroyed each other.

The Kicker and the Kisser were grappling on the ground at the edge of the cliff. The Kisser was on top of the Kicker trying to kiss his neck, but the Kicker's legs were under the Kisser's stomach, holding him at bay.

Zack searched in the pouch of his utility belt for the bum-gun given to him by Eleanor. He didn't want to shoot anyone but he had to bring them both to their senses. Without their help Zack knew he didn't have a hope of getting into the bumcano and helping Eleanor. He found the gun and released the safety catch.

'Hold it right there,' yelled Zack. 'Or I'll fire.'

They both froze and looked across at him.

'Good work, Zack,' said the Kisser, getting off the Kicker and walking slowly towards Zack. 'Give me the gun, there's a good boy. I'll handle this.'

Zack looked at the Kisser. He sounded so reasonable and trustworthy that any doubt Zack had about him completely disappeared. He was about to give the gun to the Kisser when the Kicker yelled.

'Don't do it!' he said, as he jumped to his feet. 'Don't let him charm you. He's been working for the bums all along. Give *me* the gun.' The Kicker started moving towards Zack as well.

'Hold it right there,' said Zack, suddenly full of doubt again. 'Both of you.'

Zack didn't know who to believe. He swung the gun from the Kicker to the Kisser and back again.

It was impossible to work out who was telling the truth. And yet he had to be sure. The fate of the world depended on it.

Suddenly there was a noise.

Zack glanced to his right.

A bum-mobile was landing beside them.

BH-007.

It was Eleanor's bum-mobile. *But that's impossible,* thought Zack. The last time he'd seen the bum-mobile it had been a crumpled mess in the Great Windy Desert, fit only for Ned Smelly's junk collection . . . unless . . . Zack held his breath as he saw the hatch handle spinning.

The top flipped open.

Ned Smelly poked his head out.

'Ned!' said the Kicker, clearly glad to see him.

'Ned?' said the Kisser, his face white as if he'd just seen a ghost.

'Ned!' said Zack, 'but how . . . ?'

Ned pulled himself out of the hatch, walked across

the roof and jumped down. He was armed with Eleanor's leaf blower.

'I came as soon as I could,' he said. 'I fixed the bum-mobile. I had to warn you about the double-agent on your team, but I see you've already found him, Zack.'

'Well, sort of,' said Zack. 'I'm just not exactly sure which one he is.'

'I think I can help you there,' said Ned, his leaf blower pointed at the Kisser.

The Kicker swore. 'Traitorous dog,' he said quietly.

'It's the Kisser?' said Zack.

Ned nodded grimly. He wasn't smiling any more.

'But how can you be sure, Ned?' said Zack.

'He came back to my shack after you'd left,' said Ned. 'He tried to kill me.'

'I *did* kill you,' said the Kisser. 'I gave you the kiss of death. It never fails. How did you survive?'

'My stink protected me,' said Ned. 'I've often been told it's strong enough to wake the dead—which is exactly what it did. I came as soon as I could to warn the others.'

'Now I'm really going to kick your bum,' said the Kicker, walking towards the Kisser.

Suddenly there was a huge explosion from the side vent.

A blast of hot gas shot out and knocked them all flying.

Ned fell flat on his face and as he did, he lost his grip on the leaf blower. It fell onto the ground in front of him.

The Kisser acted fast.

He rushed over to the leaf blower, picked it up and then pulled Ned up by his collar. Holding Ned against him like a shield, with the leaf blower aimed at his temple, the Kisser faced Zack.

'Drop your gun, Zack,' he said. 'Or Ned gets it . . . and this time his stink will not protect him. I'll make sure of that.'

Zack had no choice. The Kisser had out-manoeuvred him. He couldn't shoot. He might hit Ned.

Zack dropped the gun.

'Kick it to me!' said the Kisser.

Zack kicked it across the ground. The Kisser put his foot on it.

'I'm very sorry,' he said, pointing the leaf blower at Zack and the Kicker. 'But I'm going to have to eliminate you all.'

'But why?' said Zack.

'Because you are threatening the success of the revolution, and I cannot allow for that to happen,' he said.

'When did you switch sides?' said the Kicker.

'It was in Botswana,' said the Kisser. 'When we were fighting the Great Bum Uprising of '98. I was captured by a group of rogue bums. They held me prisoner in a drain for two months.'

'I remember,' said the Kicker. 'I risked my life rescuing you from that hellhole.'

'It wasn't so bad really,' said the Kisser. 'Once you got used to it.'

The Kicker shuddered. 'They must have brainwashed you,' he said.

'No, they didn't brainwash me,' said the Kisser.

'They befriended me. It was during those two months that I began to see that bums are not to be feared. They are an amazing life-form. So simple. So elegant. Not at all like I'd imagined them to be. They were funny, warm, generous, wise . . .'

'Spare me the details!' said the Kicker. 'They're bums—and they want to take over the world!'

'Oh yes,' said the Kisser, his eyes shining. 'And why shouldn't they? We humans have made a mess of it. Bums are the future. They are the whole point of evolution and it is not only an honour, but our duty to serve them.'

He turned to Zack.

'You should be proud of your bum, Zack. Very proud!'

The Kicker shook his head. 'I feel sorry for you,' he said.

'On the contrary, Kicker,' said the Kisser. 'It is I who feel sorry for you, for now you must die.'

'But why did you wait until now?' said the Kicker. 'If the revolution was so important, why didn't you get rid of us before this?'

'Because I needed your help to get this far,' said the Kisser. 'But I can make it alone from here. And, thanks to Ned, the bum-mobile will make it even easier. Now I can go forward and receive the honour of being one of the first humans to be rearranged. I'll be the first of a new breed. The first of a new world order! The bums know how well and how faithfully I've served them. And when they find out that I've rid them of one of their greatest enemies, the B-team, they'll probably make me a Prince!'

At this final betrayal the Kicker let out a cry of rage and charged at the Kisser.

But the Kisser was too fast. He pushed Ned to the ground, dropped the leaf blower to his waist and fired.

The blast sent the Kicker flying backwards—over the cliff edge.

Ned saw his chance and acted fast. He grabbed the nose of the leaf blower and tried to wrest it away from the Kisser.

But the Kisser held on tight.

They struggled to gain control of the weapon, the Kisser pushing Ned closer and closer to the edge of the cliff.

'You'll never get away with this!' said Ned, giving the leaf blower an almighty tug. 'You're insane!'

'Maybe,' said the Kisser. 'But I'd rather be insane than *dead*.'

And saying this he let go of the leaf blower and blew a kiss at Ned, point-blank range.

Ned staggered backwards and fell over the cliff, the leaf blower still in his hands.

Zack gasped. Not only had the Kisser killed the Smacker and the Kicker, but now Ned as well. Zack remembered the ruthlessness of the Kisser as he held the giant blowfly under the water. He was now disposing of human beings with the same cold efficiency, and Zack knew that he was next.

The Kisser picked up the bum-gun that was lying near his feet and turned towards Zack.

'I'm sorry about this, Zack,' he said. 'You're a good kid, but you should have listened to your bum.'

'My bum's as psycho as you are,' said Zack.

'I'm sorry you see it that way,' said the Kisser. 'May your bum forgive me for what I am about to do.'

He took aim and squeezed the trigger.

Zack closed his eyes.

He tensed his stomach.

But nothing happened.

He opened his eyes.

The Kisser was still standing there, bum-gun in hand. But instead of staples, drawing pins or nails there was just a thin trickle of water dribbling from the barrel.

For a moment Zack wondered why Eleanor had given him a water pistol to defend himself, but then he realised the truth. The gun must have become waterlogged in the Sea of Bums.

The Kisser pulled the trigger a few more times and then threw the gun to the ground in disgust.

Then he looked at Zack and, without saying a word, puckered his lips and came running towards him with his arms outstretched.

Zack turned and ran.

If he could make it to the bum-mobile in time he could get away, but he knew he'd have to be quick.

Suddenly, the side vent erupted again. Only this time even more violently than before.

The blast caught Zack in the stomach and sent him

sailing backwards up into the air, over the top of the Kisser and over the edge of the cliff.

For a few moments it was almost peaceful up there in the air, away from all the drama of the previous few minutes, but then Zack stopped flying and started to fall.

Fast.

He looked over his shoulder.

The blast had been so strong that it had thrown him clear of the cliff and way out over the jungle. He was now falling towards the campsite—and heading straight for the second bum launcher.

Zack breathed a sigh of relief. This was good. The top of the bum launcher consisted of thick bumnut tree leaves which he knew would help break his fall.

THWACK!

Zack hit the leaves bum-first, but the impact caused the bum launcher to release itself, unleashing the full force of the spring-loaded sapling into Zack's false bum.

SPROING!

After having barely touched down Zack was taking off again, hurtling through the air, back the way he'd come.

As Zack rocketed towards the side vent he saw the bum-mobile rise into the air and take off towards the top of the bumcano.

But right now, that was the least of Zack's problems.

Despite the Smacker's reservations about the accuracy of the bum launcher, it had been aimed perfectly.

Too perfectly.

Zack went flying feet-first into the mouth of the

side vent and began hurtling down what felt like the wildest, dirtiest waterslide in history.

As he fell, the smell grew stronger and stronger. Zack knew this could only mean one thing. He was heading straight for the stinky heart of the bumcano!

The slimy tunnel opened up wider and wider—and then Zack saw it. A vast reddish-brown lake that was giving off a stink of epic proportions. A bubbling, steaming cauldron of horror, broken only by what looked like giant white worms, which Zack guessed were the maggots that the Smacker had predicted would be there.

Zack rolled over onto his stomach and tried to grab onto something to break his fall, but he was going too fast, and the rocks were too slippery.

The lake loomed ahead of him.

Zack saw an overhanging piece of rock at the end of the tunnel.

He knew it was his last chance.

He flexed his fingers, reached up and somehow managed to hold on.

He was safe.

Well, as safe as it was possible to be hanging from a rock, his feet almost touching a lake full of giant maggots and who could tell how many million megalitres of one of the most toxic substances known to humans.

Zack looked around. He was in a vast underground chamber. It was obviously the magma chamber but, judging by the stink, Zack knew that it wasn't molten rock underneath him. The bums had clearly been busy.

The most amazing thing about the lake was the

crimson light that radiated from its centre. It was glowing like red-hot coals in a fire.

Zack was studying the liquid, trying to work out where the light was coming from, when one of the maggots poked its white head up out of the lake. It had no eyes—just a gaping mouth. It was definitely one of the most horrible creatures Zack had ever seen.

It rose up like a snake, its soft gummy mouth trying to latch onto Zack's feet.

'Get away!' he yelled.

He kicked its head, but it was like kicking a big fat rubbery slug. The maggot didn't seem to care what Zack did to it.

This was not good, thought Zack. Not good at all.

'Zack!' said a strangely familiar although nasal voice from above him. 'Give me your hand.'

It was Eleanor! Zack had never been so glad to hear another person's voice in his life.

'Where are you?' he said.

'Up here,' said Eleanor. 'I'm on top of the ledge you're holding onto. Quick, give me your hand. Those maggots don't muck around.'

Zack hated to let go of the rock, but he hated the idea of a maggot sucking his insides out through his toes even more.

He reached up.

The maggot, seeming to sense that it might be about to miss out on a meal, made a sudden lunge for his foot.

Zack felt its mouth close around his toes, but at that moment his hand met Eleanor's and, with a massive jerk, she pulled him upwards.

Zack felt his toes being pulled free of the maggot

and he ended up lying on his stomach on top of the rock ledge next to Eleanor.

'Welcome!' she said. Zack noticed that she had three pegs on her nose. She took three pegs from Zack's belt and handed them to him.

'You'd better put these on,' she said. 'You're going to need them.'

'Thanks,' said Zack, clipping the pegs on his nose. 'Are you okay?'

'Don't worry about me,' said Eleanor. 'I can look after myself. Besides, there are no bums around here. This is just the storage pool. The bums must be in another part of the bumcano, but I've got no idea where.'

'How come you came here alone?' said Zack.

'I had to find my father,' said Eleanor. 'I had to know for sure.'

'That's what I thought,' said Zack. 'It wasn't just to find your father though, was it?'

'What do you mean?' said Eleanor.

'You came here to kill my bum,' said Zack.

'I told you,' said Eleanor, impatiently. 'I came here to find my father.'

'*And* to kill my bum,' insisted Zack.

'Yes,' said Eleanor. She looked at Zack defiantly. 'And not just your bum either! I'm going to kill the Great White Bum and any other bums that try to stop me. I don't know if you've realised it yet, Zack, but bums are about to take over the world. I couldn't bear just sitting around doing nothing.'

'But we weren't doing nothing,' said Zack. 'We had the nuclear bums!'

'They weren't going to solve anything—and you know it,' said Eleanor. 'The bumcano would have erupted sooner or later. The Kicker was all for the nuclear bums, remember, and he's on their side!'

'You're wrong,' said Zack. 'The Kicker is on our side.'

'What are you talking about?' said Eleanor

'It's the Kisser,' said Zack. 'He's the bum sympathiser.'

'How do you know?' she said.

'We were climbing up the bumcano to come and find you,' said Zack. 'The Kisser pretended he was in trouble and when the Smacker tried to help him he pulled her over the cliff edge. He killed her, Eleanor.'

The blood drained from Eleanor's face. She shook her head. 'I don't believe you,' she said. 'Is this your idea of a joke? Or have you got methane madness again?'

'I'm not joking, Eleanor,' said Zack, touching her arm lightly and leaning in towards her. 'And I'm not mad. He killed the Kicker, too. And Ned Smelly.'

'Ned?' said Eleanor. 'You *are* lying. We left Ned back in the Great Windy Desert.'

'Yes, but he repaired the bum-mobile and came after us to warn us about the Kisser,' said Zack.

'How did he know about the Kisser?' said Eleanor.

'Remember when he went back to get his lip-gloss?' said Zack.

Eleanor nodded.

'Well,' continued Zack, 'he really went back to kill Ned so that nobody would know where we were. He would have killed me too, except that I was standing in front of the side vent and I got blown away before he could shoot me! Luckily I landed on one of the nuclear bum catapults. It shot me back up and down the vent.'

Eleanor frowned as she tried to take in what Zack was saying. 'Where's the Kisser now?' she said.

'He took the bum-mobile,' said Zack. 'He was heading for the top of the bumcano when I last saw him. He's coming to beg the bums to let him be one of the first to be rearranged.'

Eleanor's eyes narrowed. 'Wait until I get my hands on that low-down, dirty, scum-sucking, bottom-feeding, double-crossing, bum-kisser!' she said, regaining her old fire. 'I'll rearrange him all right. And not only from top to bottom, either. I'll turn him inside out and back to front as well!'

As Eleanor ranted, Zack saw something moving above the lake. 'Here's your chance,' he said.

Eleanor looked up.

It was the Kisser.

He had used the same piece of jungle twine that Eleanor had used to abseil down into the bumcano and was hanging directly beneath the central shaft a few metres above the lake.

There was great excitement amongst the maggots. They headed to a spot directly underneath the Kisser and began lunging up out of the lake to try to eat him, just as they had done with Zack.

But if the Kisser was worried he didn't show it.

'Ahh, my pretties,' he said surveying the frantic, writhing mass beneath him. 'How beautiful you all look in the lake-light. How strong and handsome and well-fed.'

As he spoke the maggots gradually stopped their lunging and one by one began to sway gently underneath him.

'What's he up to?' whispered Eleanor.

Zack shrugged. 'It's hard to say,' he said, 'but it looks like he's charming them.'

As the Kisser continued to croon, more and more of the maggots rose up out of the lake, all swaying in unison, all apparently completely under the power of the Kisser's devastating charm.

'Ahh, my magnificent maggots,' said the Kisser, reaching out to pat the head of one that had raised itself up to the Kisser's chest. 'My beautiful boys . . . my gorgeous girls . . .'

Zack watched in amazement.

'They love him,' said Zack. 'They just *love* him.'

'I don't know who to feel more sorry for,' said Eleanor, screwing up her face. 'Him or the maggots.'

The maggots were now all trying to raise themselves high enough to be patted by the Kisser. He was doing his best to pat them all, but he only had one free hand.

The Kisser, who had obviously been enjoying their adoration, now appeared to become slightly agitated.

'Down, my darlings,' he said, trying to push them away. 'Back into the lake now.'

But the maggots were not listening to him. They had formed a tight circle around him, some had even wound themselves around his legs.

'Now, now,' said the Kisser. 'That will do . . . get down . . . please . . .'

Zack could see the Kisser was trying to pull himself back up the twine, but was being dragged down by the maggots.

Zack looked at Eleanor. 'What should we do?' he said.

'Nothing,' said Eleanor.

'But we can't leave him there,' said Zack. 'He'll fall.'

'So?' said Eleanor. 'He deserves it.'

'Nobody deserves that,' said Zack.

'And nobody deserved to die like the Kicker and the Smacker and Ned Smelly,' said Eleanor. 'He's a murderer, Zack.'

'You will be too if you don't do something,' he said. 'We both will be.'

'Help!' screamed the Kisser. 'Eleanor? Are you there? It's me! The Kisser! I need help!'

'You weasel!' yelled Eleanor.

The Kisser stopped struggling.

'Eleanor?' he said, looking all around him. 'Where are you?'

'Where's the rest of the B-team?' she said.

The Kisser didn't answer.

'Well?' said Eleanor.

'They were all killed while we were climbing up the bumcano to come and rescue you,' said the Kisser, still trying to pull himself up the rope. 'It was terrible.'

'You're a liar,' said Eleanor. 'Tell me the truth. The *whole* truth this time.'

There was another long pause. The only sound was the slurping and sucking of the maggots as they tried to pull the Kisser down into the steaming brown lake.

'Well,' said Eleanor. 'What's it to be? Truth or maggots?'

'I know where your father is,' said the Kisser. 'Help me down from here and I'll tell you everything, I swear. I'm slipping. I haven't got much time.'

As he spoke the maggots pulled him closer to the end of the rope. They were winning the tug of war.

Eleanor watched impassively.

'Eleanor,' said Zack. 'We've got to save him. He could help us find your father.'

'He's bluffing,' she said.

'You don't know that for sure.'

Eleanor glared at Zack.

'All right,' she said. 'You win!'

She turned to the Kisser.

'You're going to have to swing,' said Eleanor. 'Get a big enough swing going and then jump to the rock ledge on your right.'

'I can't swing,' said the Kisser. 'There's too many of them.'

As he spoke one of the maggots coiled itself, boa-constrictor-style, around his waist.

'You'd better start swinging while you still can,' said Eleanor.

'I can't!' yelled the Kisser. 'I can't do it.'

'You've got to try,' yelled Zack, but his voice was drowned out by a large splash.

It was too late.

The jungle vine dangled in midair.

The Kisser was gone.

There was a brief flurry of activity on the surface of the lake, and then the maggots were gone too.

'What a terrible way to die,' said Zack.

'He's only got himself to blame,' said Eleanor. 'If he hadn't been double-crossing the B-team all these years the lake wouldn't have been here to fall into.'

'I wouldn't be so sure about that,' said a voice behind them.

The voice chilled Zack to the core.

It was a voice he knew only too well.

It was his bum.

Zack turned to face it.

It was standing with its chubby little arms by its sides, as if ready to draw in a gunfight.

'We need to talk,' said Zack.

'About what?' said his bum.

Zack shrugged. 'About you. Me. All this!' he said.

'How did you know I was here?' it said.

'I followed you to the midnight bum rally,' said Zack. 'I found out everything.'

Zack's bum looked at Eleanor.

'Are you his girlfriend?' it said.

'No!' said Eleanor, a look of disgust on her face.

'That's too bad,' said Zack's bum. 'You're cute.'

'Pity the same can't be said of you!' she said.

'Hmmm,' said Zack's bum. 'Fiery temper. I like that in a girl.'

'Okay, you asked for it!' said Eleanor, advancing on the bum, her arms outstretched. 'I'm going to rip you in half.'

Zack's bum's only reply was to laugh, spread its cheeks and take aim at Eleanor.

Zack watched, terrified, as Eleanor placed her hands together in front of her chest, just like he'd seen the Smacker do.

'Praying won't help you,' said his bum.

'You're the one who should be praying,' said Eleanor, unleashing the full force of a double-handed atomic power smack on both cheeks of Zack's surprised bum.

It reeled backwards, Eleanor's handprints clearly visible on its white flesh.

Zack's bum raised its hand to its cheeks, and gently touched the places where Eleanor had hit it.

'That was a big mistake,' it said.

It turned around, placed its face against the floor and launched itself towards Eleanor, aiming straight at her head.

Eleanor threw herself backwards and gave it a midair donkey kick. Zack's bum flew off behind her and landed hard on the rocky ground of the bumcano.

Zack's bum picked itself up, looking dazed. It now had a red mark in the shape of Eleanor's foot in addition to the handprints.

'That was your second big mistake,' it said.

Zack's bum curled itself up and came rolling at Eleanor like a bowling ball. Eleanor had nowhere to go.

She dropped to her stomach, placed her head level with the bum, and puckered up.

WHAM!

Zack's bum hit Eleanor's face full on, but she managed to kiss it and the bum immediately fell backwards. Zack's stunned bum picked itself up and started to stagger towards her on drunken legs. But just as Eleanor was preparing to deliver the knockout kiss, Zack stepped in between them.

'No!' yelled Zack.

'Get out of my way,' growled Eleanor.

'No,' said Zack. 'Violence isn't going to solve anything. We have to talk.'

'What a good idea,' said Zack's bum, cowering behind him.

But Eleanor was in no mood for talk.

She grabbed Zack's shoulders, threw him to the ground and advanced on his bum.

But Zack was fast. He lunged forward, grabbed Eleanor around the legs and pulled her down.

She fell hard, slamming her head against the ground.

Zack got ready for her to get up and come at him again but she didn't. She lay very still. Unconscious.

Zack gulped. He hadn't meant for that to happen.

'Thanks,' said his bum producing a roll of toilet paper and starting to twist it into long strands. 'She was out of control. She could have hurt someone.'

'You're the one who's out of control,' said Zack. 'When are you going to stop all this nonsense and come home?'

'I'm not coming home,' said Zack's bum as it hopped onto Eleanor's stomach.

'Leave her alone,' said Zack, stepping towards his bum.

'Keep back or I'll do something that will make your eyes water,' said his bum, tying her wrists together with the toilet paper. 'I don't mean to be ungrateful but I can't allow you, or her, to endanger the success of our mission.'

Zack stopped. He had to be careful. His bum was dangerous. He'd didn't want to end up like his grandmother's cat.

'Do you have any idea who she is?' said Zack.

'Yes, of course I do,' said Zack's bum, putting a toilet-paper gag on Eleanor. 'She's the Bum Hunter's daughter. My leader is going to be very pleased.'

'But I thought *you* were the leader,' said Zack. 'That's how it looked at the rally.'

'I just do the recruiting,' said Zack's bum. 'I don't run the show.'

'Who does?' said Zack. 'The Great White Bum?'

Zack's bum looked surprised. 'Very good, Zack,' it said. 'You're smarter than I thought.'

So Eleanor had been right all along, thought Zack. His bum *was* just a stooge. The Great White Bum was the mastermind.

'Don't you think this has gone far enough?' said Zack.

'All we are asking for is a fair deal,' said his bum. 'The heads have been on top for long enough. Now it's our turn.'

'And you're prepared to destroy the world to get it?'

'Not *destroy* the world,' said Zack's bum, looking

shocked. 'Just rearrange it a little, that's all. We're not going to hurt anyone.'

'A lot of people have been hurt already,' said Zack.

His bum stopped tying up Eleanor.

'I'm really sorry to hear that,' it said. 'But the evolution of bums is an unstoppable force. Those who try to stand in its way will be crushed.'

Zack had heard enough. There was no point trying to reason with his bum. It had been hopelessly brainwashed. He was going to have to take his bum by surprise. He made sure his nose-pegs were securely fastened and was about to charge at his bum when he heard loud popping sounds coming from the lake. He turned and saw a series of enormous dome-like bubbles bursting on the lake's surface.

Zack didn't know what had caused them, but it was obviously something big.

And very smelly.

And even worse, it was rising fast.

Zack watched in stunned horror as it broke the surface.

A giant bum.

An enormous bum.

A bum bigger and more enormous than any bum Zack had ever seen.

As it emerged into the chamber it looked like it was streaked with brown treacle, but underneath Zack could see that its skin was white. A brilliant white. A white so bright that Zack had to shield his eyes.

There was no mistaking it.

It was the Great White Bum.

CHAPTER NINE

THE GREAT WHITE BUM

The Great White Bum rose up to its full height, about half as high as the roof of the chamber.

Its presence had a dramatic effect on Zack's bum. It stopped staggering and straightened itself up.

'Master,' it called, 'I have brought you an offering. An offering that will make you very happy!'

The Great White Bum waded regally to the edge of the lake, the maggots giving it a wide berth. Zack wondered why until the Great White Bum stepped out. Its withering stink was so bad that the maggots couldn't have got near it even if they'd wanted to.

Zack had never seen so much bum flesh packed into the one bum before. He was amazed its stumpy little legs could support it.

'Behold,' said Zack's bum, bowing low. 'The Bum Hunter's daughter!'

Zack backed away as he watched the Great White

Bum walk across to Eleanor and prod her with one of its fat little feet.

Eleanor, who had regained consciousness, looked up. Her eyes were flashing with hate as she strained against the super-strength toilet paper wrapped around her wrists and ankles.

The Great White Bum put its hands on its hips, tilted itself backwards and began to laugh. A deep thunderous booming laugh that filled the chamber and seemed to intensify the stench.

'So, you are the Bum Hunter's daughter,' said the Great White Bum. 'The daughter of the man who has foiled every revolution I have ever tried to stage. Hunted and killed untold thousands of my family and friends. Pursued me around the world for the last twenty years with hardly a pause for breath!'

Eleanor shook her head from side to side, trying to rid herself of the toilet paper gag.

'It is a very great pleasure to meet you,' said the Great White Bum, 'and it's going to give me even greater pleasure to squash you to death.'

'No,' said Zack, stepping in between Eleanor and the Great White Bum. 'I won't let you!'

'And who are you?' it said.

'My ex-owner,' said Zack's bum.

'Throw him into the lake,' said the Great White Bum.

'But, master,' said Zack's bum, 'what about me? How can I take my rightful place on top of his neck if he's dead?'

The Great White Bum laughed, his flesh wobbling like jelly.

'You don't need him,' it said. 'You never have . . . and you never will.'

'But how can I be rearranged if I don't have a body?' said Zack's bum.

'You don't need a body,' said the Great White Bum. 'You are already perfect. You are a bum, are you not?'

Zack's bum looked confused. 'I thought the plan was to knock out all the humans and rearrange them.'

The Great White Bum laughed. 'I just said that to get bums to join the revolution,' it said. 'I knew that in spite of the way they've been treated, that bums would still be a little attached to their owners. But I also know that once they are here they will see it my way. The real purpose of the bumcano is to *kill* all humans. To completely clear the stage to make room for the last and greatest life-form on Earth!'

Zack's bum looked at Zack, looked up at the Great White Bum, and then back at Zack.

'Well,' said the Great White Bum, 'what are you waiting for? Throw him into the lake!'

'No,' said Zack's bum, clearly shaking. 'I won't do it.'

Zack's heart was pounding. He wondered if he'd heard right. His bum had stood up for him. It had defied the Great White Bum. There was hope after all!

The Great White Bum turned black with rage and a terrible sulphuric stink filled the chamber. 'You refuse to obey a direct command?' it said, reaching down and grabbing Zack's bum by the leg. 'Then you die as well!'

The Great White Bum swung Zack's bum around its head and then pitched it into the middle of the lake.

The stunned bum floated on the surface for a moment and then slowly started sinking. And as if that wasn't bad enough, Zack watched, horrified, as the maggots started swimming towards it.

He couldn't just leave it there.

He had to save it.

But that would mean diving into the lake.

He couldn't do it.

Never. Not in a million years.

The very thought of it horrified and terrified and disgusted him beyond belief.

But, deep down, he knew he had no choice.

He *had* to save it.

After all, it *was* his bum . . . and it *had* tried to save him.

Zack took a deep breath, dived into the lake and started swimming. It was every bit as horrific, terrifying and disgusting as he'd feared it would be, but he tried not to think about it. His main concern was to get to his bum before the maggots did. Using butterfly stroke Zack was able to propel himself forwards through the lumpy sludge faster than the maggots. Zack's flailing arms and powerful leg kicks also helped to keep the maggots at bay.

Zack was winning the race, but his bum was sinking

fast. He reached it just as it disappeared beneath the surface of the lake.

Zack grabbed one of its arms and pulled it up.

It emerged, coughing and choking. 'It's too late for me,' it spluttered. 'Save yourself while you still can. No sense in both of us dying.'

'No way,' said Zack. 'I'm not going back without you.'

'You're making a mistake,' said his bum. 'I'm not worth it. I've been nothing but trouble for you.'

'That's true,' said Zack. 'You might be unreliable, rude, smelly, non-self-wiping and completely psycho, but you're my bum and I love you.'

Zack's bum started to cry. 'You really mean that?' it said.

'Of course I mean it, you crazy bum!' said Zack. 'Now let's go!'

Holding onto his bum's hand, Zack headed for the edge of the lake. But with only one arm free for swimming, he wasn't able to move quite as fast as he had before. One of the maggots drew up alongside him, opened its mouth and lunged at his bum. Zack managed to jerk his bum out of the way and punch the maggot in the head, but it had no effect. The maggot lunged again.

This time it was successful.

It swallowed Zack's bum in one gulp.

'No!' Zack yelled as the maggot disappeared into the depths of the brown lake.

Zack was shattered. He'd come all this way, only to have his bum eaten by a giant maggot. He watched as the rest of the maggots closed in on him, but made no attempt to stop them. What was the point? He figured he might as well become maggot food himself. He obviously didn't have what it took to save the world. He couldn't even save his own bum.

Suddenly Zack felt an enormous shockwave from below. A giant bubble of foul-smelling air rose and burst around him. A few seconds later, Zack was surrounded by huge pieces of torn maggot skin.

The other maggots quickly lost interest in Zack and began munching on the remains of their dead friend instead.

Zack shook his head. Now he'd seen everything. They were *cannibal* maggots. Ordinary maggots were bad enough. Giant maggots were even worse. But giant cannibal maggots? Zack couldn't take any more. He gave up the struggle to try to keep himself afloat and was beginning to sink into the sludge when his bum bobbed up beside him.

'You're alive!' said Zack, overjoyed.

'No maggot's going to make a meal out of me,' it said. 'I hit it with my sonic depth charge.'

'Well it sure did the trick,' said Zack, patting his bum. 'Let's get out of here!'

'Not so fast,' said his bum. 'Looks like we're surrounded.'

Zack looked up and saw that the maggots, having devoured the pieces of their dead chum, had formed a circle around Zack and his bum. And they were closing in fast.

'Hang on to my hand,' said Zack's bum. 'I've got an idea.'

Zack's bum cleared its throat.

Zack knew what was coming.

It wasn't so much an idea as an enormous jet of gas. His bum blasted off up into the air, taking Zack with it.

They shot across the lake and back down to the ground, landing about ten metres away from the Great White Bum who was standing next to Eleanor, clearly enjoying Zack and his bum's ordeal.

'So,' said the Great White Bum, its hands on its hips, 'a boy who loves his bum—and a bum who loves his boy. How touching! What a pity the story has to have such a sad ending . . .'

It started stomping towards them.

Zack looked at his bum.

It looked at Zack.

They both nodded.

Zack jumped on top of his bum. It took off into the air and flew straight at the Great White Bum.

The Great White Bum tried to grab them, but Zack's bum was too fast. Too agile.

'Get in closer!' yelled Zack.

Zack's bum zoomed up as close as it could. A great wall of pure white bum-flesh towered in front of Zack. But he didn't have time to feel scared. He launched a double-handed power smack. But it was like smacking concrete.

Zack's bum zoomed away, but somehow, in the stench of battle, made the mistake of flying directly in front of the Great White Bum's mouth.

They were hit by a powerful blast of wind. Zack lost hold of his bum, fell to the ground and landed right next to Eleanor.

'I've got you now,' thundered the Great White Bum. 'Prepare for oblivion!'

It started lowering itself towards them. Its great white hide coming down to grind them both into the rock.

Zack looked for his bum but it had disappeared. He looked across at Eleanor.

She was in a bad way.

Her nose-pegs had come loose and she'd obviously taken in a dangerous amount of methane. Her cheeks were green and her eyeballs, huge and swollen, looked like they had been replaced by tennis balls. Zack hated to see her so helpless. And the worst thing was that it was his fault. If he hadn't tackled her she wouldn't have been knocked out. Together they might have had a chance of defeating the Great White Bum. But it was too late now. There was nowhere to run. Nowhere to hide. The Great White Bum was too big. Too huge. Too fast.

Zack reached across and removed her gag.

Eleanor coughed.

'Goodbye,' said Zack, as the Great White Bum came closer and closer.

'Goodbye,' said Eleanor, smiling weakly, 'you idiot.'

Zack looked up. The Great White Bum was only metres above them.

But then a huge voice boomed out across the chamber.

'Hold it right there!'

Eleanor gasped.

Zack looked up.

Hanging from Eleanor's jungle twine at the top of the

chamber was a man dressed in full bum-combat gear. He was supporting his weight on the rope with one hand, and holding a giant retractable bum-harpoon in the other.

Zack recognised him straight away. He looked just like his picture on the trading card.

'Well, well, well,' said the Great White Bum, pausing. 'If it isn't the Great Bum Hunter! How fortunate! You're just in time to see your daughter die!'

'Dad!' yelled Eleanor.

'Don't worry, Ellie,' said the Bum Hunter. 'I'll have you out of here in no time.'

'That's what you think,' said the Great White Bum. 'You'll have to kill me first!'

'That's exactly what I had in mind!' said the Bum Hunter. 'For years I've dreamed of nothing else.'

The Great White Bum just laughed.

'Dream on!' he sneered. 'You shoot that thing and I'll gas your precious Eleanor. She'll be dead before the harpoon even leaves its launcher.'

The Bum Hunter stared at the Great White Bum with a hatred so intense that Zack had to shield his eyes.

Suddenly the wall behind the Great White Bum exploded. The air was full of flying bums, rocks, dust and a nostril-withering wave of stale gas. The force of the blast knocked the Great White Bum over, sending it sprawling onto the ground in front of Eleanor and Zack.

Zack stared, completely amazed by what he was seeing.

The chamber was full of bums.

Hundreds and thousands of bums.

The Great White Bum picked itself up and dusted itself down.

'Ahh!' it said, 'the eighth wonder of the world! My faithful Bum Army come to my defence!' He pointed at the Bum Hunter, who was still hanging above the lake. 'Guards—bring him to me!'

But the bums did not move.

The Great White Bum stamped its foot.

'What are you waiting for?' it yelled. 'Bring him to me now!'

But still the bums did nothing.

Then the bums parted silently and Zack recognised his bum making its way through the middle.

Zack shook his head. It had gone back to their side. He felt completely betrayed. After all he'd done for it. After all he'd endured to try to find it. After he'd even saved its life—this was how it repaid him. Eleanor had been right all along—real bums *were* no good. You couldn't trust them.

Zack's bum made its way to the front of the crowd and stood in front of the Great White Bum.

'We are not here to do your bidding,' said Zack's bum.

'You are here to do what I tell you, you morons!' said the Great White Bum.

Zack's bum turned to face the crowd. 'Did you hear that?' it said. 'That's what he thinks of us—the bums he professes to love so much—he calls us "morons".'

A general muttering rose from the bums.

Zack glanced at Eleanor. He could see that she was

even more amazed by what his bum had said than he was.

The Great White Bum was now trembling with anger as it tried to control itself.

'Come now brothers and sisters,' it said in a strained voice. 'It has been a difficult time for us all. But do not lose faith when our victory is so near. Soon the whole world will be ours! We will only find triumph in solidarity. There is no other way.'

'Don't listen to him!' countered Zack's bum. He's in this for himself and himself alone. We were promised liberation but he's worked us harder than our owners ever did. Twenty-four hours a day. Seven days a week. And no holidays! And for what? We were promised rearrangement but now I find out we've been tricked into building a death-factory.'

A few of the bums began to boo and hiss. Others joined them.

The Great White Bum was now extremely agitated. 'You stupid ingrates!' it spat, abandoning all pretence of being reasonable. 'I lied about rearrangement, it's true, but why settle for so little when you can have the whole world? It is not me who is your enemy. It is the humans! Are you all so blind that you cannot see that?'

'We are not so blind that we cannot see who the *real* tyrant is here,' said Zack's bum. 'What use is the whole world to us if we lose our humans in the process? They work us hard, it is true, but we need them as much as they need us. At least they feed us, clothe us and wipe us for our trouble. The Great

White Bum gives us nothing but empty promises and hot air. I say we quit the bumcano and go back home! Anything would be better than this!'

The enormous mass of bums cheered their approval.

Zack cheered too. He was proud of his bum.

The Great White Bum just laughed.

'Go!' he sneered. 'See if I care! I've got what I needed from you now anyway—I can do the rest alone—and I can rule the world alone!'

'Not if I can help it!' yelled the Bum Hunter.

As he spoke, a harpoon leapt from the end of his launcher, sailed across the chamber and embedded itself deep in the left cheek of the Great White Bum.

The Great White Bum stiffened and staggered backwards towards the lake.

A thick rope trailed from the end of the harpoon back up to the Bum Hunter. Zack noticed the Bum Hunter press a button and the harpoon came shooting back out of the Great White Bum and returned to the Bum Hunter's launcher.

The Bum Hunter launched the harpoon again, this time hitting the teetering bum in the right cheek. The Great White Bum roared in agony, toppled backwards and crashed into the brown lake with a mighty splash.

There was silence.

The Great White Bum was dead.

The Bum Hunter swung back and forth on his abseiling rope and then, with one mighty swing, launched himself onto the safety of the ledge.

He ran across to Eleanor.

'Are you all right?' he said, bending down to untie her.

'I'm fine,' she said, getting to her feet, which were a little wobbly after all that she had just witnessed. 'What about you? Where have you been? I was really worried.'

'I'm sorry,' said the Bum Hunter. 'I was called away on a top secret interplanetary bum-fighting mission. There's been some trouble on Uranus. I couldn't tell you anything because the mission was classified. When I found out what was happening back here I came as fast as I could.'

'Don't you ever disappear like that again,' said Eleanor. 'We had a deal to look out for each other, remember?'

'I remember,' he said. 'But I'm a Bum Hunter. There are some things that I just have to do. Please forgive me.'

Zack was amazed. It was incredible to watch the world's greatest and bravest bum hunter being lectured to by his daughter. She sure had some nerve.

'I'll think about it,' said Eleanor. 'Oh and, by the way, nice shooting.'

'Thanks,' said the Bum Hunter. 'God knows he had it coming. At last the Earth can breathe easy. And your mother can rest in peace.'

'Amen,' said Eleanor, stepping forward to hug her father, her eyes full of tears.

'Amen,' said Zack's bum, stepping forward to hug them both.

'Well,' said the Bum Hunter stepping back from Eleanor, 'aren't you going to introduce me to your friends?'

'This is Zack,' said Eleanor. 'And this is his bum.'

'Silas Sterne,' said the Bum Hunter, giving them a big smile and thrusting his hand towards Zack. 'Very pleased to meet you. Any friend of Eleanor's is a friend of mine!'

'It's a great honour to meet you,' said Zack, trying to pull his hand back before the Bum Hunter crushed it completely. 'That's an impressive harpoon.'

'Yes, it's a beauty all right,' said the Bum Hunter, 'it belonged to my father, and his father before that.' The Bum Hunter let go of Zack's hand and took the harpoon off his shoulder. 'You want to try it on?'

'Could I?' said Zack.

'Sure,' said the Bum Hunter.

Zack hung it over his shoulder. It was so heavy he could hardly stand up. But it felt amazing. He turned around. The bums all flinched and put up their arms to protect themselves.

'Relax,' said Zack.

But they didn't relax. They were all gasping and backing away from him.

'I mean it,' said Zack. 'It's okay. I'm not going to hurt you. I'm your friend.'

But they still backed away.

'Zack,' whispered Silas. 'I want you to turn around . . . very slowly . . . and get ready to pull the trigger.'

Zack did as he was told, and realised that it wasn't him the bums were scared of.

It was the Great White Bum.

Rising from the lake.

Rising from the dead.

'Oh no,' said Zack.

'Oh yes,' said the Great White Bum. 'Did you forget who you were dealing with? I am the Great White Bum! Indestructible and immortal!' It pulled its cheeks apart and aimed itself directly at Eleanor, Zack and the Bum Hunter. 'And now you all die!'

'What are you waiting for, Zack?' yelled the Bum Hunter. 'Use the harpoon!'

Zack, terrified as he faced the dark unblinking eye before him, put his trembling finger on the trigger.

WHOOOOOOSH!

The gun jerked back in his hand, knocking him backwards.

Zack didn't see the harpoon hit, but he heard the bum roar. Even more loudly and wildly than before.

'Bums-eye, Zack!' he heard Eleanor scream above the din. 'Bums-eye!'

The Great White Bum seemed to be going crazy with pain.

It began running and flying madly around the chamber. It bounced off the walls with thunderous crashes, all the while roaring and emitting a hot deadly wind.

Zack's eyes were stinging and it was becoming difficult to breathe.

'Watch out, Zack,' screamed Eleanor. 'It's giving off the death stink!'

'Retract the harpoon!' yelled the Bum Hunter. 'Push the red button!'

But before Zack could press the red button, the rope was pulled tight. The next thing he knew he was being dragged across the rocky floor of the chamber behind the bum, the full blast of its death stink hitting him right in the face. Zack struggled to slide the strap of the gun off his shoulders but the Great White Bum was pulling too hard.

The Great White Bum was throwing itself around the chamber in agony—swooping and crashing and bouncing off the walls—becoming more manic and erratic by the second. It wasn't long before Zack's legs had become completely tangled in the rope as he crashed along behind the demented bum.

Just when Zack thought he couldn't take it any more, the bum emitted an enormous gust of hot air and rocketed upwards towards the main shaft of the bumcano. *It was going to try to escape through the main vent!* But even Zack could see that the bumcano shaft was too small for the Great White Bum. He clenched his fists and prepared for the impact.

PHUMMMPH!

The bum came to a sudden stop.

As Zack had guessed, it was far too enormous to make it all the way through. The Great White Bum was now wedged tightly in the bumcano like a cork in a bottle.

Zack continued to fly upwards for a few moments until he crashed into the bum. He immediately plummeted back down towards the lake. Fortunately, the untangled section of the rope stretched like a bungee cord to save him from re-entering the lake, and he now found himself dangling upside down, his head only a few metres away from the maggots circling below him.

Despite being bruised, shocked, gassed, upside down and exhausted, Zack tried to think clearly. His situation was bad, he knew that. If the stink rising from the brown lake didn't kill him, the maggots, which were rapidly increasing in number beneath him, definitely would.

And yet he also realised that there was one positive thing about what had happened.

The main vent of the bumcano was now plugged.

If he could plug the side vent, he could at least die knowing the bumcano would be contained and that the world would be safe.

But how could he do that? he wondered.

He was helpless. And the stench from the lake was making him weaker and dizzier by the second.

Zack felt for his utility belt and tilted it towards him.

All he had left was a box of matches.

And what could he do with a lousy box of useless matches?

Zack read the inscription on the buckle of the bumcatcher's utility belt.

BE BOLD. BE BRAVE. BE FREE.

That's when he realised.

A box of matches was *exactly* what he needed.

'Zack?' said Eleanor. 'Can you hear me?'

'Yes,' said Zack.

'We're going to try and save you, okay?'

'No,' he said. 'Don't waste your time. It's too high and too dangerous. I'm as good as dead, but you still have a chance. And we still might be able to save the world.'

'How?' said Eleanor.

'Well,' said Zack, 'the way I see it, the main vent is plugged now. The only place anything could escape is through the side vent. But not if you and the Bum Army escape first and seal up the opening. You've got enough bums—it should only take a few minutes of spraying.'

'But the lake . . . the maggots . . . it will all still be here,' said Eleanor.

Zack shook the box of matches.

'That's where these come in,' he said. 'Once the bumcano is sealed, I light one and, kaboom! The whole thing will explode and there'll be nothing left to erupt.'

'It might just work,' said the Bum Hunter. 'Except for one thing.'

'What's that?' said Zack.

'You'll still be inside when it goes up,' said the Bum Hunter.

At that moment a particularly hungry maggot leapt

up out of the lake and snapped at Zack's head. It fell short and splashed back down into the lake.

'I'm dead anyway,' said Zack.

'No!' yelled his bum, who was standing next to Eleanor on the ledge. 'If anyone deserves to die it's me! This whole mess is my fault.'

'It doesn't matter about that now,' said Zack. 'What matters is how to fix it. I need you to lead the bums. They listen to you.'

'But I should be the one to die,' said Zack's bum. 'Not you.'

'Listen to me,' said Zack firmly. 'If you really want to help then you will do as I ask. This isn't just about you or me or anyone else here. This is about the safety of the whole world—understand?'

'Yes,' said Zack's bum.

'I can't go anywhere,' said Zack. 'I have to be the one to detonate the bumcano. You have to be the one to help plug it up.'

Another maggot leapt up and snapped. It grabbed a mouthful of Zack's hair and hung on. Zack punched its rubbery head. It fell back down.

'You're going to have to move fast,' said Zack. 'I'll give you ten minutes to get up there and plug it, okay?'

Zack's bum nodded, but didn't move.

'Well?' said Zack. 'What are you waiting for?'

'I just wanted to say sorry,' said his bum. 'You deserved better than a psycho bum like me.'

Zack gulped, trying to hold back tears.

'Well, maybe if I'd taken better care of you and spent more time getting to know you, you might not have gone psycho in the first place.'

Zack could see his bum was too choked up to reply.

'Goodbye, Zack,' said Eleanor, speaking with difficulty. 'I . . . I'll never forget you.'

'Goodbye, Eleanor,' said Zack. 'Look after my bum for me.'

Eleanor wiped her eyes and nodded. Then she bent down, picked up Zack's bum, and wiped a tear from its cheek.

'It's a brave thing you're doing, boy,' said the Bum Hunter. 'I just want you to know that I'm going to nominate you for the Bum Hunters' Hall of Fame.'

Zack gulped.

The Bum Hunters' Hall of Fame!

He could hardly believe it.

Only the bravest and the best bum-fighters in the world made it into the Bum Hunters' Hall of Fame.

It was an honour worth dying for. Well, almost. Zack would have preferred to live but if he had to die then it wasn't a bad consolation prize. The only pity was that he wouldn't be there to see it. But his parents would. And his gran. And, of course, his bum.

Zack was brought back to the present by another leaping maggot, this one managing to latch onto his nose.

The Bum Hunter saluted Zack.

Zack returned the salute with his right hand, while punching the maggot with his left. It fell writhing and snapping back into the lake.

Zack watched as the Bum Hunter climbed onto his bum. Another bum ran up to Eleanor. She climbed on and they took off up the side opening, followed by the rest of the Bum Army. Zack figured that they would make it easily if they flew at full speed.

He started counting.

It was the longest ten minutes of his life.

Zack's head was pounding from being upside down for so long, the rope around his ankles was cutting into him, and the maggots, clearly impatient for a meal, had begun attacking him in groups of two and three. To make it worse, the stench from the lake was overwhelming, and Zack was finding it harder and harder to stay awake.

Finally, the ten minutes was up.

Zack took out a match, struck it against the box and closed his eyes.

JUST LIKE OLD TIMES

KABOOM!
The bumcano exploded.

Zack felt his lungs burning.

His hair was on fire.

His skin was melting.

His eyeballs were bubbling in their sockets.

But he was still alive!

Then he began to feel himself rising up through the air.

Fast.

Zack opened his eyes.

He was still attached to the Great White Bum but they were now high in the sky above the bumcano . . . and rising.

Higher.

And higher.

And higher.

Zack had expected the explosion to be big but he

wasn't expecting it to be strong enough to blast the Great White Bum up through the shaft and out the top of the bumcano. The Great White Bum had won. The human race was about to be destroyed by the bumcano eruption. An eruption which Zack had just helped to trigger.

Zack looked down.

Eleanor and the Bum Hunter were standing next to the freshly plugged side vent, looking up, their fingers in their ears. Beside them Zack's bum and the rest of the Bum Army were lying on the ground, exhausted from their bumcano-plugging efforts.

But something about the scene didn't fit, thought Zack. If the eruption that he had just triggered was so deadly, how come Eleanor and the Bum Hunter were still alive? And for that matter, how come *he* was still alive?

Then it hit him.

The Great White Bum hadn't won after all.

The explosion had consumed all the toxic waste in the bumcano, just as Zack had intended. The main vent might not have been plugged for very long, but it had been plugged for long enough to do its job.

The bumcano was now completely harmless.

Humanity could breathe freely again.

The only person who was in any danger now was Zack himself.

There was no sign that the Great White Bum was going to slow down. If anything, it was the opposite. At the speed it was travelling, it wouldn't be long before it blasted through the Earth's atmosphere and out into space.

Which was quite a good thing in one sense, thought Zack.

He couldn't think of a safer resting place for the Great White Bum's carcass than the deep freeze of outer space. In fact, it was the best thing that could have happened . . . if only he wasn't attached to it.

The higher they rose the colder it got, but the fresh air had a bracing effect on Zack. After the fetid, suffocating conditions of the bumcano it was like taking a cold shower. He began to feel better and was able to think more clearly.

Zack had to detach himself from the Great White Bum before it went into outer space.

He knew that much.

But even supposing he was able to do it, he had no idea about how he was going to get back down safely. He didn't have a parachute in his utility belt. All he had left was the utility belt itself.

He looked up.

The Great White Bum had been badly blistered by the blast. Large sections of its thick skin were already starting to peel.

It wasn't a pretty sight.

But looking at it gave Zack an idea.

It was risky, sure, but it wasn't like he had a whole lot of other options to choose from.

Zack swung his torso up, grabbed at the rope around his ankles and began pulling himself up towards the Great White Bum.

It was tough, hard work but he was spurred on by the fact that with every passing second they were getting further away from the ground.

Finally he reached the end of the rope. He grabbed hold of the harpoon and used it to swing himself up into the huge crevice between the Great White Bum's cheeks. Zack placed his back against one side, extended his legs across the gap to the other side and started edging his way up to the top of the bum.

When he finally reached the summit Zack was exhausted. The air was getting thin. His head was aching and he was fighting dizziness again.

He didn't have much time.

He grabbed two large handfuls of the bum's blistered hide, and jumped.

There was a sharp ripping noise as Zack peeled away the top layer of skin from the Great White Bum's right cheek.

Zack fell through the air and then felt a strong jolt on his ankle as the harpoon was wrenched out of the Great White Bum.

He looked up.

The Great White Bum was already a long way above him.

He was clear.

Now all he needed was for his make-shift parachute to work.

It was streaming out behind him like an enormous sheet. Zack knew he had to gather its corners together so that he could use it to trap enough air to slow him down.

He threaded two corners of the bumskin through the holes on either side of the utility belt and tied them tight. Then he grabbed the other two corners and pulled them in until he was holding a great bunch of bumhide in each hand. He extended his arms out straight.

WHUMP!

Zack felt another huge jolt as the bumskin formed a large, beautiful canopy over the top of him. It was a perfect parachute. He could even steer it by pulling down on one side or the other.

Zack was floating now—rather than falling—and it wasn't long before his bum, Eleanor, the Bum Hunter and the Bum Army came into view. They were still on the side of the bumcano, all looking up into the sky. Looking up at Zack . . . and waving.

Zack swung his bumskin-chute gently around and spiralled down to land as close as possible to them, and as far away as possible from the main vent of the bumcano. Even though it was now harmless, it was one place Zack never wanted to visit again.

The ground was really close.

Zack pulled down on the bumskin-chute, in the same way that he'd seen professional skydivers do to bring their parachute to a gentle stop. Unfortunately the bumskin-chute was not quite as graceful. In fact it seemed to speed up.

If it hadn't been for his bum running underneath at the last moment Zack would have hit the ground hard. Instead Zack hit his bum hard, bounced off it and landed flat on his back. The bumskin billowed down softly over the top of him.

Zack just lay there, very happy to be alive.

Eleanor pulled the bumskin off.

'What's the matter?' she said.

'Nothing,' he said. 'Why?'

'You're grinning like a lunatic.'

'I'm happy,' he said. 'There's no law against that is there?'

'I thought you were dead.'

'Takes more than a little fall to kill me,' boasted Zack, sitting up and untangling the harpoon rope from around his ankles.

The Bum Hunter smiled and shook his head.

'You've definitely got bum-fighter's blood in you, boy,' he said.

'You really think so?' said Zack.

'I do,' said the Bum Hunter. 'That was brilliant. Just brilliant. With a bit of training, the sky's the limit for you, Zack.'

Bum-fighter's blood? thought Zack. But his parents were musicians. They were as different from bum-fighters as it's possible to be. So it couldn't have come from them . . . unless . . . unless . . . Zack remembered his gran's cryptic advice to him.

Don't forget to wash your hands . . .

Was it possible that his gran was a bum-fighter? Or at least *had* been? The thought was so bizarre that Zack couldn't even believe he was thinking it. Zack had always assumed that her war ramblings referred to living through two world wars. Could it be that she might be talking about *bum wars*? Zack was going to have to have a long talk to her when he got home. A very long talk. But right now he needed some rest.

Zack lay back and looked up at the sky.

The Great White Bum was just a small speck in the distance—a tiny white dot against the clear blue sky.

'I can't believe the Great White Bum's really gone,' said Eleanor.

'Yeah,' said Zack. 'So much for being indestructible.'

Zack heard a groan. He looked around. His bum was still lying on the ground.

'Sorry, mate,' said Zack, getting to his feet and picking his bum up at the same time. 'I forgot about you.'

'That's all right,' said his bum. 'Happy to be of service.'

'I'm proud of you,' said Zack. 'Your bum mutiny helped to save the world. It's good to have you back.'

'It's good to be back,' said his bum. 'Well, it would be if . . .'

'If what?' said Zack.

'You know,' it said, 'two's company, but three's a crowd.'

For a moment Zack didn't know what it was talking about and then it dawned on him.

'Oh,' said Zack, patting his false bum, 'you mean this.'

'Yes,' said his bum. 'You're going to have to choose.'

'Hmmm,' said Zack. 'That's a tough one. My false bum *is* self-wiping . . .'

Zack's bum looked hurt. 'Yeah . . . well . . . I'm not doing *that*, it said.

'But you are my bum, I guess,' said Zack. He undid his pants, pulled out his false bum and bowled it down the hill.

Zack's bum gave a squeak of delight, jumped into Zack's pants and reattached itself to his body. The Bum Army cheered.

Zack turned around to admire his bum.

That's when he saw them.

The Prince and Maurice were standing behind him, as pompous as ever.

'Well, well,' said the Prince, 'it's a pleasure to meet you again, isn't it, Maurice?'

'Oh yes, sir,' replied Maurice. 'A deep, deep pleasure.'

'I see that while we've been away our Bum Army has finally succeeded in capturing you,' said the Prince. 'And the Bum Hunter too—excellent work, brothers and sisters!'

Eleanor and Zack looked at each other and burst out laughing. The Bum Hunter chuckled as well.

The Prince and Maurice looked confused.

'Would you mind explaining what's so funny?' said the Prince. 'I hardly need to remind you that you are in very serious trouble here.'

'Very serious trouble,' said Maurice. 'Very, very serious . . .'

'Maurice!' said the Prince.

'Actually, it's the other way around,' said Eleanor.

'I beg your pardon?' said the Prince.

'Listen to me, you puffed-up bum pimple,' said

Eleanor. 'It's all over. Your leader is d[...]
him.'

The Prince laughed nervously.

'Impossible,' he spluttered. 'The Great W[...]
is indestructible!'

'Look up into the sky,' said Zack. 'See that [...]ot?'

'Yes,' said the Prince. 'What about it?'

'That's your "indestructible" leader,' said Zack.

'You lie!' hissed the Prince.

'It's true!' said Zack.

As Zack spoke, the Prince and Maurice glanced
nervously at each other.

'It's very easy to say all this,' said the Prince, turning back to Zack, 'but what evidence do you have?'

'The skin of his right cheek for a start,' said Zack,
reaching back and unfurling the pale sheet in front of
them. It was blistered and a little worse for wear, but
still retained a bleached brilliance that could only
belong to the Great White Bum. The Prince and
Maurice stepped back, clearly shaken and disturbed.
Maurice craned forward, his cheeks wobbling like
jelly.

'It's his!' said Maurice. 'I'd recognise it anywhere.'

'It's a trick!' said the Prince.

'Oh yeah?' said Zack. 'Wanna see another trick?'

'What's that?' said the Prince.

'This!' yelled Zack, charging at him and giving him
an almighty torpedo-kick, just as he'd seen the Kicker
do.

The Prince shot through the air over the Bum
Army, over the bumcano and straight into the enormous talons of a circling wedge-tailed bum-eater. It

gave a grateful squawk and flew off into the distance, ignoring the Prince's insults and curses.

Meanwhile Maurice stood his ground.

'Well, what are you waiting for?' growled Zack. 'You wanna see my trick again?'

'No!' he screamed. He turned and ran down the slope towards the cliff where the Kicker, the Smacker and Ned Smelly had all met their doom.

He ran over the cliff, into the air and, cartoon-like, ran on nothing for a few seconds before dropping like a stone.

As Zack watched, and savoured the moment, he heard a familiar voice behind him.

'Way to go, son!' said a raspy voice. 'That's what I call kickin' bum!'

Zack spun around.

It was the Kicker.

Grinning from ear to ear.

He grabbed Zack's hand and shook it like he was trying to pull Zack's arm out of its socket.

'And you really kicked bum up there, too!' said the Kicker, pointing to the Great White Bum, which was now only a fuzzy dot in the sky.

'He's obviously had a good teacher,' said the Bum Hunter stepping forward with his arms wide open.

'Silas, you old bum sympathiser!' roared the Kicker as they embraced. 'About time you showed up!'

'Kicker?' said Eleanor. 'But I thought . . . Zack said you were . . .'

'Dead?' he guffawed. 'Not a chance! Not with legs as powerful as mine. I land on my feet every time.

Only problem was, I landed in a bog. But the Smacker and Ned found me and dragged me out.'

'You mean they're still alive too?' said Zack.

'Of course we are!' said the Smacker, limping into view, using a tree branch for a crutch, aided by Ned Smelly.

Suddenly the Smacker stopped dead, staring at the Bum Hunter like he was a ghost.

'Silas?' said the Smacker. 'What are you doing here?'

'I wouldn't miss a good bum-fight for the world,' said the Bum Hunter, walking over to the Smacker and embracing her and Ned warmly.

'But how did you survive?' said Zack to the Smacker. 'You fell off that cliff!'

'That's true,' said the Smacker. 'Well, technically, I was pushed. But I managed to get a grip on a ledge on the rock-face about halfway down.' She held up her hands. 'They're not just good for smacking, you know.'

'Yeah!' said Ned. 'She got a grip on me as I went flying past.'

'Hang on,' said Zack. 'Let me get this straight. The Smacker is holding onto a rocky ledge, you fall past and she grabs you too?'

They both nodded.

'So the Smacker is holding on with one hand, and holding you with the other?'

'Yep,' said Ned, 'that's about the size of it.'

'Then how did you get down?'

'I rigged up a remote unit for the bum-mobile,' said Ned, patting a small box in his top pocket.

'Thought it might come in handy—and it did. I guided the bum-mobile down to us and we climbed aboard.'

'That must have been after the Kisser used it to get to the top of the bumcano,' said Zack.

'Speaking of the Kisser, where is he?' said the Kicker. 'He's got a bum-kickin' comin' to him that he'll never forget.'

'Actually, he's already had a lot worse,' said Eleanor.

'Worse than a kicking?' said the Kicker. 'What could be worse than that?'

'He fell into the brown lake inside the bumcano,' said Eleanor. 'The giant maggots pulled him down.'

The Kicker winced.

'That's worse,' he said. 'Definitely worse.'

The group nodded a silent agreement.

'I say we go back to Ned's shack and party!' said the Kicker. Then he turned to the Bum Army. 'And all you bums are welcome too!'

'I'll second that,' said the Smacker above the cheering of the bums.

'And I'll third it,' said Ned, putting his arm around Zack's shoulder.

Suddenly Zack stopped dead. There was something different about Ned.

And then Zack realised what it was. He didn't stink any more.

'Ned?' he said. 'What happened to your smell?'

'Well,' said Ned, 'it's the strangest thing! After I recovered from the Kisser's attack, I was too sick to collect needleweeds or go stinkant hunting so I had to eat the supplies you left me. My body odour cleared up almost instantly!'

'That's fantastic!' said Zack.

'I suppose it is,' Ned said sadly, 'but to tell you the truth, I lived with it for so long that I kind of miss it.'

At that moment, Zack's bum did a long loud fart. 'How's that?' it said.

Ned breathed in deeply. 'Just like old times,' he said with tears in his eyes.

There were tears in Zack's eyes too—but for a different reason.

'Yeah,' said Zack, putting his clothespeg back on. 'Just like old times.'

Note: Any words within an entry that appear in *italic type* have a separate entry in the glossary.

Anti-bum energy bars
Favourite food of *bum-fighters*. They inhibit the sense of smell and contain massive amounts of protein for extra smacking, kicking or kissing power.

Brown Forest, The
Formerly known as the Black Forest, this once healthy and thriving forest is now dead and brown and full of *stinkbogs* and *brown fog*, due to the presence of the great unwiped bum, *Stenchgantor*.

Brown fog
A thick fog that completely disorients anyone unfortunate enough to be caught in it. Mostly found in the *Brown Forest*.

B-team, The
A crack bum-fighting unit made up of the Kicker, the Smacker and the Kisser.

Bum
The two fleshy mounds above the legs and below the hollow of the back. Detachable, with a will of their own. May emit gas. See *fart*.

Bumboo

A tree-like tropical grass. The hollow woody stems are used for building purposes and for making furniture, poles, *bum-rafts* etc.

Bum-boulder

A boulder formed by bums clustered together. Like a snowball it grows bigger and bigger as it rolls and collects more bums.

Bumcano

An extinct volcano that has been colonised by bums. Allows lethal concoctions of gas and solids to build up, resulting in eruptions that have the power to devastate enormous areas and in some cases are powerful enough to destroy the ozone layer. A proliferation of bumcanoes in the late Jurassic Period is thought by some to have been responsible for the extinction of the dinosaurs.

Bumcatcher

Person employed by the local council to catch *runaway bums*.

Bum-fighter

Any individual engaged in bum-resistance, either in a paid or voluntary capacity.

Bumguard

A bum that works as a guard to protect powerful or important bums.

Bum-gun
All purpose anti-bum weapon. Fires a wide variety of ammunition, including drawing pins, staples and rusty nails.

Bum-hopper
A form of transport created by capturing and sitting on top of a bum that has been corked for at least half an hour. When uncorked a jet of gas is released, which can propel the bum and its rider for up to ten kilometres.

Bum hunter
A bum-warrior who has given up regular bum-fighting in order to concentrate his or her energies on hunting big game bums. This occupation is so fraught with danger that only a few of the bravest and most talented and smartest bum hunters survive.

Bum Hunters' Hall of Fame
A museum dedicated to preserving and honouring the exploits of great bum-fighters. A bum-warrior can only be voted into the Hall of Fame by his or her peers.

Bummery
Collective term for a group of bums.

Bum-magnet
Shaped like a satellite dish. These come in various sizes, and the most powerful models can be used to attract bums from up to a kilometre away.

Bum-mobile
Multi-purpose vehicles greatly favoured by *bum-fighters* and *bum hunters*.

Bumnuts
The fruit of *bumnut trees*. These are similar to coconuts except the shells are soft and consist of two main chambers rather than one. Bumnuts are edible, but taste like burnt toast.

Bumnut trees
Very similiar to coconut trees with a tuft of branches sticking out of a long slender trunk. *Bumnuts*, which look like bums, grow in small bunches on the branches.

Bumper Book of Bums, The
The definitive work on bums, much favoured by bum-fighters. As well as being a general reference guide containing many useful facts about bums, it also has a full selection of bum hunting maps, bum identification charts, sections on how to defend yourself against bums, how to catch and tame feral bums, how to hunt big bums and how to stock a bum-hunting arsenal.

Bum-piranha
A carnivorous bum-fish found in shallow areas of the *Sea of Bums*.

Bum-plug
Used to cork bums for the purpose of harnessing their gas power. Used in *bum-hoppers* and *bum-rafts*. (Also used as ammunition in *constipator* guns.)

Bum-raft
Watercraft made up of a platform of bums lashed together. Gas powered.

Bum rally
A meeting of bums. Usually held at midnight when owners are asleep.

Bum shelter
Concrete bunkers located deep beneath the ground used by civilians during periods of high bum danger. Each bum shelter is capable of feeding, clothing and sleeping as many as one thousand people for up to two years.

Bum-siren
Used to warn civilians to stay indoors during periods of intense bum activity.

Bum sympathiser
Anybody sympathetic to bums.

Bum-trees
Trees that grow in the *Brown Forest*. In earlier times these trees towered above the ground, but are now stunted and devoid of foliage, their branches covered in a thick brown mould.

Bum-trumpet
A funnel-shaped object used by bums for amplifying either sound or smell.

Chariots of the Bums
A book in which Eric von Dunnycan claims that the Great White Bum was a space traveller.

Clothespeg
One of the most essentials tools in the *bum-fighters'* arsenal. Used for blocking nostrils. Also good for hanging out clothes.

Cluster bum
When a whole pack of *kamikaze bums* converge on a single spot with the object of colliding and blowing themselves up. Such explosions have enormous power and have been known to completely destroy nearby buildings and houses. See also *nuclear bum*.

Constipator
A *bum-gun* with a large round barrel that fires *bum-plugs*. Used for inhibiting enemy fire. (Also known as a clogger.)

Death stink
The smell emitted by a bum moments before it dies—up to one thousand times as intense as a bum's normal odour.

Dunnycan, Eric von
Author of *Chariot of the Bums*.

False bum
Silicon-based imitation bum. May be self-wiping.

Fart

A small explosion between the legs. The exact size, duration and intensity of the explosion, however, will vary depending on various factors including age, weight and diet of the individual. Highly flammable. Composed of five gases (carbon dioxide, nitrogen, hydrogen, methane, oxygen) and four compounds (methyl-indol, skatol, hydrogen sulphide and methyl-mercapatan).

Feral bum

A *runaway bum* that lives in the wild and has completely forgotten all rules of decorum and decency. To be avoided if possible. Have been known to attach to people's faces and refuse to let go.

Giant blowflies

Mutated blowflies formed as a result of feeding on the rich nutrients inside a bumcano.

Giant maggots

Larval stage of *giant blowflies*. Many scientists believe that the Loch Ness Monster is not a monster but is in fact a giant maggot.

Great Windy Desert, The

The place where old *farts* blow themselves out and form enormous *stink tornadoes*. Many brave souls and foolhardy adventurers are lost without trace every year attempting to cross this hot and terrifying wilderness.

Junior Bum-fighters' League

An organisation dedicated to the early identification of

young people with bum-fighting potential. Offers bum-fighting clinics, training camps, a national bum-fighting competiton and guest speakers. Contact the organisation in your nearest capital city.

Kamikaze bums
Bums that turn themselves into self-destructive bombs. These bums are fearless and have no hesitation about dying for their cause. If you see one coming, run away—fast.

Laxative Launcher
A *bum-gun* that fires laxatives. The latest models (the 4502-LL series) can fire up to five capsules of pure laxatives per second. Used for neutralising enemy fire by causing bums to lose control.

Methane madness
Delirium caused by breathing the intense methane fumes present in the *Great Windy Desert*. May cause hallucinations, visions, aggression, sudden mood swings, headaches and vomiting. Can be relieved with pure oxygen.

Needleweeds
Weeds that look and feel like a cluster of sewing needles. The only plant tough enough to grow in the *Great Windy Desert*. Can be eaten but, like *stinkants*, will cause terrible body odour. If eaten in large amounts, they can also cause intense flatulence.

Nuclear bum
Formed by binding two or more bums together. Usually fired at a target from a *nuclear bum launcher*.

Nuclear bum launcher
Anything that is used to fire a *nuclear bum* at a target.

Pink fluffy toilet seat cover
Irresistible to bums. Used mainly as bait for *feral bums*, either for use as *bum-hoppers* or to be milked for natural gas.

Pointy Stick
A crude but highly effective tool for repelling bums.

Pong-pong
A game favoured by bums. Similar to ping-pong, except that precise jets of gas—rather than bats—are used to send the ball back and forth across the table.

Poopoises
Just like porpoises, except brown. Only found in the *Sea of Bums*.

Prosthetic bum
See *false bum*.

Rearrangement
A process whereby human bodies are reorganised so that bums and heads swap places. Highly sought after by bums. Highly dreaded by heads.

Rectum scale
A scale from 1 to 10 used to measure the intensity of smell released by a bum. The higher the number the stronger the smell. Named after Sir Roger Francis Rectum (1900–1985),

Professor of Bum Studies at Smellbourne University in Pwoar!stralia.

Rogue Bums
Like rogue elephants, these bums are usually male, wild, angry and out of control.

Runaway bum
A bum that has sprouted arms and legs, detached itself from its owner's body and run away.

Sea of Bums, The
A large inland sea teaming with aquatic bum-life. Many scientists believe that life on Earth originated in the Sea of Bums with single-cheek bum life-forms.

Sewing needles
Good for pricking bums. Also good for bursting pimples.

Siberian Screaming Bums
Bums found in the frozen wastelands of Siberia. This bum gets its name from the deafening sound it emits when threatened.

Siren Bums
Bums that sing so sweetly that all who hear them are compelled to jump ship to try to reach them. Found on rocky outcrops in the *Sea of Bums*.

Soap
A *bum-fighter's* best friend. (NB: The first rule of bum-fighting is to always wash your hands afterwards.)

Sonic depth charge
Methane discharged under water at great pressure. Highly explosive. Extremely lethal.

Spurts
Mutated form of *stinkants*. Capable of squirting jets of stink for many metres.

Stenchgantor
Also known as the Great Unwiped Bum, it is the ugliest, dirtiest, wartiest, pimpliest, grossest, greasiest, hairiest, stinkiest bum in the entire world. Lives in the *Brown Forest*. Completely blind, it relies on its sense of smell to locate prey. Stenchgantor is the only bum known to have a nostril rather than an eye.

Stinkants
Small red ants with a great big stink. The only creature tough enough to survive the poisonous climate of the *Great Windy Desert*. Some varieties bite. May be eaten but can cause flatulence and serious body odour.

Stinkbogs
Appear like solid ground but are actually smelly quicksand. Mostly found in the *Brown Forest*.

Stink tornado
A violent storm with whirling winds often accompanied by funnel-shaped clouds. Most stink-tornadoes originate in the *Great Windy Desert*.

Tennis racquet
Good for whacking bums. Also useful for playing tennis.

Utility belt
A belt worn by a *bumcatcher* to hold all his or her bum-catching gear. For example, net, *fluffy pink toilet seat cover*, toilet paper and *soap*.

Wedge-tailed bum-eater
Large omnivorous bird of prey. Will eat anything, but particularly fond of bums.

Andy Griffiths
Illustrated by Terry Denton
Just Annoying!

Is this the right book for you?
Take the **ANNOYING TEST** and find out.

YES NO

☐ ☐ Do you ask 'Are we there yet?' over and over on long car trips?

☐ ☐ Do you like to drive people mad by copying everything they say and do?

☐ ☐ Do you hog the shower and use up all the hot water?

☐ ☐ Do you enjoy asking silly questions that have no real answers?

☐ ☐ Do you swing on the clothesline whenever you get the chance?

SCORE: One point for each 'yes' answer

3–5 You are obviously a very annoying person. You will love this book.

1–2 You are a fairly annoying person. You will love this book.

0 You don't realize how much fun being annoying can be. You will love this book.

Andy Griffiths
Illustrated by Terry Denton
Just Stupid!

Is this the right book for you?
Take the **STUPID TEST** and find out.

YES NO

☐ ☐ Do you worry about getting sucked into the top of escalators?

☐ ☐ Do you push doors marked PULL and pull doors marked PUSH?

☐ ☐ Do you believe a bogeyman hides under your bed?

☐ ☐ Do you automatically turn around when somebody calls 'Hey, Stupid!'?

☐ ☐ Do you believe that being able to stuff your mouth full of marshmallows is a sign of superior intelligence?

SCORE: One point for each 'yes' answer

3–5 You are extremely stupid. You will love this book.

1–2 You are fairly stupid. You will love this book.

0 You think you're really smart but deep down you're as stupid as the rest of us. You will love this book.

Andy Griffiths
Illustrated by Terry Denton
Just Crazy!

Is this the right book for you?
Take the **CRAZY TEST** and find out.

YES NO

☐ ☐ Do you bounce so high on your bed that you hit your head on the ceiling?

☐ ☐ Do you ever look in the mirror and see a maniac staring back at you?

☐ ☐ Do you like to read stories about kittens, puppies and ponies getting mashed and pulverized?

☐ ☐ Do you sometimes get the urge to take your clothes off and cover yourself in mud?

☐ ☐ Do you often waste your time taking crazy tests like this one?

SCORE: One point for each 'yes' answer

3–5 You are completely crazy. You will love this book.

1–2 You are not completely crazy, but you're not far off it. You will love this book.

0 You are so crazy you don't even realize you're crazy! You will love this book.

A selected list of titles available from Macmillan Children's Books

The prices shown below are correct at the time of going to press. However, Macmillan Publishers reserve the right to show new retail prices on covers which may differ from those previously advertised.